I0779466

PINKIE PROMISE WE WON'T DIE

PINKIE PROMISE WE WON'T DIE

BY ALEXA SUAREZ V.

Library of Congress Control Number: 2024902424

ISBN: 979-8-9900183-1-0

*A special thanks to my dystopian-loving teenage self,
and my brother who shared my love for it.
I hope you like this one.*

I

The Capture

I remember. I remember them knocking on the door. I remember the way my mother's expression fell into sudden fear as she looked through the peephole. I remember the way she clutched her fist and bared her teeth as she turned back to us. The way her face relaxed in an effort to appear completely calm when, in fact, our world was about to tear us apart.

We were just kids.

The three of us stood eye to eye frozen in place almost as if we were all thinking the same thing. Not a single movement was made until I looked to the side and saw my younger brother sharing the same facial expression I had on. Fear. Uncertainty. A mixture of both.

A second knock then follows.

Quickly, my mother grabs both of our wrists and drags us down the wooden hallway. After what happened last time, we knew the safest option was to hide in her bedroom rather than in the kitchen cabinets.

"Hurry." My mother urges, rushing us into the closet.

Another knock hits the door a little more violently.

Out of panic, my mother scampers around and grabs some of the clothing from the closet. She chucks most of it to the side of her messy bed. The sheets were somewhat drawn back; the pillows were piled on the ground, and the drapes made the room darker than it was. On her nightstand was a cereal bowl left from yesterday morning that she had yet to wash, along with a blue mug with red lipstick stains on the side.

The only neat thing in her room was her bookshelf. The wooden bookshelf looked in perfect condition with its glossy grey paint as new as it could be. Each book was placed accordingly based on its size. It was my mother's prized possession. Her only escape from reality and mine, too. If only we could jump into these books and hide away in a magical land where we could feel safe.

Boy, that would be great.

Another knock hits hard against the door, startling all of us.

She gives a final sigh and approaches the closet. Up to now, I was only able to see the back of her head until the dark locks of her hair shifted ever so slightly that I could see the look on her face. Completely scared and desperate. Veins popped out of her forehead with her eyebrows furrowed below it. There was something about the way her jaw tightened with each knock from the door.

For a brief second, she tried to compose herself, but I could see it in her eyes that she was far from control. When her eyes stared intensely at mine, I felt as if they were saying something that couldn't escape her lips. Anything.

Quickly her gaze shifts and softens every so subtly meeting my brothers. Having them side by side, one can note how they look so alike — the caramel color of their skin, the bright green eyes, and the curliness of their hair.

They share an unspoken nod before she glances at me once again, this time saying 'Take care of him' before she turns on her heels and locks the door, leaving us inside the small closet with just enough space for us to be one arm's width apart.

Bang!

Another knock echoes throughout the house.

I take a deep breath and feel my brother in front of me flinch. With his other hand, he shakily clutched a baseball. It is something he always did whenever he felt nervous or scared. He would always take the baseball with him whenever he took a test, had a game, went to the doctor, and when he heard the sounds of thunder. I always thought of him like a cat, since he disliked loud noises and was easily frightened.

I place my hand on his shoulder, reassuring him that they won't find us. We share a simple nod and wait silently in the closet until we hear another bang.

In response, my mother yells "I'm coming!" in the most aggressive manner.

Eeeerrkkkkk!

The door seemed to have slammed vigorously open, judging by the sound. The hinges must've fallen off again after the way they brutally opened it last time. At least now they had the audacity to knock.

"WHERE ARE THEY?" A voice booms against the walls.

"I sent them out last week," she shouts back at the officer loud and clear.

Of course.

It's them—the G.C.P.O.A., also known as the Governmental Child Patrol Officer Association. I could go on and on about them, but now wasn't the time.

With a silent gesture, my brother points to the call, catching my attention away from the crevices of the closet door. He demonstrates in front of me by placing his ear against the wall for optimal auditory range. I smile in approval and follow his lead. Past the wall, we hear another pair of shuffling boots coming from what appears to be in the kitchen — CLASH, BANG, CLASH. They composed the sound of plates, pots, and pans slamming the tiles. The second voice murmurs along the lines of, "The children are not in the kitchen".

"Check the rooms." The first male voice yells again.

I glance at my brother with his trembling hands, one clamping against his mouth and the other still holding the baseball. It wasn't until I saw him that I realized I was doing the same thing. We take another deep breath and brace ourselves for their entrance.

You can only imagine the amount of anxiety that rose to our cheeks when the footsteps against the wooden floors made creaks of what appeared to be thick heavy leather boots. The closer it sounded, the louder my heart pounded against my chest. With our heads still against the walls at all times, it no longer felt cold. The body heat shared between me, and my brother, became one with the closet. From the tip of my fingers, I felt myself beginning to sweat profusely. My brother took note and wiped his forehead.

The anticipation was killing both of us.

With my mother's most beautiful clothing dangling over our heads, it no longer felt cozy without her in them. Yet, the smell held me grounded when I felt my knees ready to buckle and collapse. In the background, I hear the door of my mother's room slam open. My brother and I jumped, careful to not make out too much of a reaction. We were afraid to make a single move in fear that the floorboards below us would expose our hiding spot with one wrong step.

"Where are you?" The deep voice sent chills down my spine. My brother looked like he was about to lose it.

"It's okay." I mouth, reassuring my brother once more. My eyes must've adjusted to the dark closet because I was able to see his facial expressions. There were tears in his eyes, there was no doubt about it. His mouth was almost not present by the way his lips tightened, and on his cheeks was the slightest stream.

All it takes is one noise. One whisper. One sudden movement and we were goners.

Thankfully, my mother rushes into her room and says, "They're not here. You've searched the house countless times! Now get out!"

Almost. Just almost.

I see the door handle move the slightest bit before it retreats to its locked position.

"What's behind this door?" asks the officer.

In the most sarcastic voice, I hear my mother snarl back, "The closet."

My brother and I share a smirk at my mother's sarcasm. Even behind these clothes, I can feel my mother's personality. The scent of her closet matched well. It was bold and strong yet left a warm feeling in your nose.

He takes three slight steps back away from the closet. A sense of relief made me believe that this was going to be over soon.

But it wasn't.

"A closet huh." We hear a click on the other side of the door.

I know for a fact that it wasn't the doorknob, but a weapon.

"What are you doing?" My mother's voice grows warily.

I turned to my brother and saw his face filled with sheer panic. His hands became fully clutched at his sides, pale and quaking. I lift my hands ever so soundlessly to grab my brother's shoulder.

I shove him against the wall, creating space between us with only my arm in the way.

BANG! A single light shines where the bullet makes a hole.

My ears were ringing, and my head was pumping with adrenaline. My brother stood there shocked, almost as if he spotted a ghost. His eyes were searching into mine for some kind of answer. He always did that when he didn't know what to do and wanted me to help him. I wanted to look away. I wanted to tell him that I didn't know this time.

Too much was happening, so much that I had barely noticed where the bullet had hit.

At first, I didn't feel anything. My mind was spinning too much for me to understand what was happening. For a moment, the world just stopped spontaneously. It was the feeling of not knowing how to feel. Not knowing if everything was just a dream.

Within seconds, my brother's weak knees gave out as they buckled and fell along with his entire body. The ball he kept an ever-so-tight hold on, loosened out of his grasp, bouncing eagerly to the floor, rolling right at the tip of my white fuzzy socks. Both sounds of his body and ball dropping revealed our hiding space.

Another bullet rings, and this time the door is now open. In front of me stands a large man holding a gun in the palm of his hands, along with one strapped across his chest. His eyes were a bright grey, his hair was completely gone, and his face held a smirk of satisfaction. He made the type of facial expression where the predator has found their prey.

He was the fox, and I was the bunny.

I look to the side and see my mother with tears streaming down her face and forcibly crouched to the floor. Next to her was the other officer holding her back from us. I glance at my brother and see him completely lying on the floor. He was perfectly fine.

But I wasn't.

I glanced at my arm, which was completely soaked in blood. If it wasn't for my sleeveless shirt, I wouldn't have even noticed where the blood was dripping from. There, close to my shoulder, lays the bullet glistering within me.

I didn't know what to do.

I quickly peeked at my brother and bolted to the door. Or so I thought. It was a weak and stupid approach because soon after, the officer with a strained face grabbed me by my hair and held me down by the shoulders.

I hear my mother scream.

I don't remember exactly what she said. It was all a blur. It might've been my name. Or my brothers. Or simply cries. It was all too sudden and too much for me to remember. All I knew was that her screams grew faint and had anger, frustration, and fear as each word quivered and became unsteady among her protests. Her body thrashed like a hungry zombie as the officer tried to pull her down.

"This shouldn't hurt," the officer whispers in my ear.

He pulls out a needle and injects it straight into my neck. Even with my arm bleeding by my side, I still couldn't say anything. I was completely speechless. It was almost as if they had cemented my mouth shut.

Whatever was in that serum must've been strong enough to sweep me from consciousness because from there, everything became even more disoriented than before. My eyes grew heavy until all I could see was the scruffy old face of the officer in front of me. If I wasn't so unsteady, I think I would've punched that smirk off his face just like how my father taught me.

As my body gave out, the last thing I felt was my head crashing onto the floor.

My mother…my brother… If only I hadn't closed my eyes and hit my head, I would've seen what happened to them.

When I opened my eyes, I found myself in a bedroom that looked exactly like mine, only much newer. The bed sheets that I was lying on were exactly like the ones I had. It is completely soft and fluffy but holds no sentimental value, unlike my old one, not to mention the picture of my favorite cartoon character Steven the Dog is bright and colorful, instead of dull. I looked down under the covers and saw I was wearing baby-blue prison-like clothing.

The baby blue jumpsuit fit me perfectly, almost too perfectly. It's baggy enough to allow me to stretch my body and manageable enough to run if I ever needed to. The material felt very lightweight. On my feet are normal white socks and an ankle band like the ones I saw prisoners wear on TV. The band itself was so thin that I couldn't even feel it. In fact, had I not looked at my feet, I wouldn't have noticed I was wearing it. It felt as if there was a piece of paper wrapped around my skin. Each time I tried to take it off, I would get zapped.

It hadn't crossed my mind what I was wearing last time. But it was definitely not this.

When I tried to lift myself out of bed, it was at that moment when I felt a shooting pain. "Ouch!" I yelped. I lifted the mid-length sleeves of my jumpsuit to see how bad it was.

It's pretty bad.

They completely covered my upper arm and shoulder in large patches and bandages. If I were to estimate, it seems like the bullet had hit the upper part of my arm close enough to my shoulder. I was lucky to move it. Obviously, I wasn't a doctor or anything, but I knew the bullet was one centimeter away from taking away my mobility. Any idiot who was in my place could make the same conclusion.

I debated on whether I should lie here and pray I'd wilt away like a flower or investigate my surroundings. One option seemed increasingly tempting than the other.

I need to find Maxine. I think to myself guiltily.

I inhale a deep breath and work my way to lift myself.

It took a few moments, but I eventually got myself in a stable position to open the door facing the opposite side I was standing at. Next to me is a brand new pair of baby blue tennis shoes, exactly my size. I put them on and explore.

Everything is almost a replica of my house. The wooden floor panels are the same but without scratches. The halls have blurred photos of the portraits of what once were our family photos. The door frame next to my room was missing the height measurements that I had written over with a marker. All the special details of what was once my home were eradicated into something new and improved. What got me the most was the smell. The air did not smell like home but rather that of disinfectant spray. It's all just too eerie for me to not notice these subtle differences.

"Max, where are you?" I shouted as I ran to what was supposed to be his room. Everything was there. All his toy cars. His collection of signed baseballs, all of which seemed new. His messy hand paintings. The posters of his favorite race car drivers. His small stuffed animal of a zebra, ever so perfectly positioned, sat there staring at me on his bed. It's all there. Except for him.

Next, I ran into my mother's room. It was the same thing. I could no longer smell the scent of my mother. Her perfume was wrongly sprayed everywhere. It didn't *feel* like her.

I didn't bother looking back.

They glued the windows shut and completely blacked them out. None of the doors that lead outside of the house opened, preventing me from leaving the inside of this supposed house.

Feeling trapped like a mouse in a glass cage, I grabbed a chair and tried throwing it at the door, which resulted in me hurting my shoulder even more. I must've ripped something because underneath my clothing was a small patch of blood on my arm. I looked down and saw the mess I made. Scraps of the wooden chair flew everywhere.

How pathetic can I be?

Another surge of pain went up to my arm, causing me to fall to the floor. At that point, I didn't feel like getting up anymore. My body felt sore beyond belief, and everything seemed to be futile. All I wanted to do was to just sink into a puddle and drown in it.

As I lost myself in my thoughts, the door behind me opened with a click, and entering it was a nurse. As I was about to stand up, the door immediately closed from behind her.

Just terrific.

"You really shouldn't be doing that to yourself."
She scolds me. Her Russian accent reminded me of that
one substitute I had when my second-grade teacher was
sick.

The nurse had her dark hair tied into two tight side
buns, and her complexion was as pale as a white lily. She
had a very petite face, just like her neck. Her cheeks were
the color and shape of two bright red hearts, and her nurse
hat had an image of a small bear. The cartoon bear was
probably to bring some appeal to us kids.

I, on the other hand, was less amused by her
uniform.

She looked very petite and had brawny arms that
bulged out of her side. Her physique was quite slender,
yet oddly muscular in some parts.

I raised my eyebrow at her and took a step back.
"Where am I? Where's my mom? M-m-my brother?" My
heart starts to quickly race with my thoughts. I picked up
a large piece of wood from the broken chair and pointed
the sharp end directly at her.

She snorts at my gesture and inches closer to me.
She grabs the sharp end and snaps it instantaneously like
some sort of superhuman.

"Just calm down," she says, grabbing my other hand.

Calm down? Definitely. Let's all have a jolly time and have a cup of tea while we are at it! Hell, Steven, the Dog, would find this insane.

She inches closer to me, but I take another step away.

"Okay, Elena, if you calm down," she pauses for a moment. "I will explain everything. You can even see your brother," she negotiates.

I had to believe her. I didn't have any choice. It's not like I knew how to fight this woman. Especially with my useless arm.

She gestures to me in my room and follows me with a cart right beside her. I sat down, watching her intensely. She wrings out a bunch of medical equipment, a few I recognize.

"I am going to look at your shoulder," she tells me right before her hand lightly touches it. She then tells me to unzip the top part of the jumpsuit just so that she can see my arm and shoulder a little more clearly.

I unzipped it enough to where my shoulder and left arm were out in the open and gazed at my bandages. I had not even noticed that I was wearing a bra underneath until I saw the strap. Even if it was just my shoulder and my arm, I felt bare and embarrassed.

I had never worn one until now. My mother and I were supposed to have "the talk" this week about me becoming a "growing girl" and all that before I entered the seventh grade. She even had a set of training bras picked out for me to wear. Of course, I never really felt like wearing them. It just felt too weird, too strange, and just too awkward for me to handle. I knew all the standard stuff, but realistically, I had no clue what my body was like. I didn't think I would need to wear a bra just yet until the seventh grade when it was time to change into the locker rooms at school.

School.

Another lost memory.

It was like any other day, that is, until they barged in, and called Amanda to stand up. A group of tall men wearing black and red uniforms stood right in front of us with straight faces. My teacher, Ms. Robinson, was as pale as a ghost. Her hands were clutching the desk with such severity that I was almost sure that a piece of wood was chipped off.

When I first saw Amanda being taken away from the G.C.P.O.A. we were all scared. She kept screaming about wanting to see her parents and begged the teacher to take her home. She didn't want to leave with them. No one did. After her next was John. Charlie. Mona. Christopher. The list goes on.

Before I could see half of the class gone, one day, my mother decided that we weren't going back to school. That's when the G.C.P.O.A. started knocking on the doors. Taking away children from every house. Separating families apart. This was all their fault.

"Ouch," I say to the nurse. She had a cotton pad in one hand and a Q-tip in the other. Both had blood on them.

"Sorry. They got you in deep." She lightly dabs the cotton ball on my shoulder. The room completely reeked of rubbing alcohol. Next, she pulls out a long needle with green fluid. It looked like the same stuff they injected into Max's arm when he had broken it. I have no idea what was in it, but soon enough, his arm became as good as new within a few days. He didn't even need a cast.

"Almost done." She re-bandages my arm and hands me a new baby blue jumpsuit.

"Where's my brother?" I ask her bluntly.

She gives me a sigh and sits down right next to me. From the cart, she pulls out a small box and presses the top of it. Out came a small holographic man wearing nothing but white clothing.

"Hello child, do not be afraid for I am Cedric, your mobile introducer to project Code 11-Z" he continues with a disclaimer, "Until further notice, any child under the age of 18 will or eventually will be in our care and responsibility. That includes you."

The mini hologram man points at me and continues. "Now you may be wondering, what is going on? Well, fear not, Cedric is here to explain." He smiles and fades into a video.

Standing there was a family of five: a mother, a father, two daughters, and a son. "Here is a family. They are the Thompsons." The picture then transitions to a warehouse where the mother and father are working on packaging a box. "The Thompsons are currently working at a shoe warehouse. They work here for very long hours a day to help feed the family." The image then shifts into a different setting.

I look at the nurse in confusion. She doesn't make any eye contact with me and continues to look at the tablet. "Now, because of problems like the economy, there needs to be more work! More work equals more money!" he cheers. "By having kids like you in our care, Mr. and Mrs. Thompson will be able to work more hours!"

A puff of confetti spouts out of nowhere. To conclude, the projection then shows the parents smiling straight at the camera. Behind them are metal bars and a playground where the children are playing.

The blue-figure guy pops up out of nowhere and points at me once again. "You are currently located in one of the billions of care divisions of Crinx United." Before I can freak out, the tablet lifts into the air and scans my face with a blue light.

"Thumbprint requested," the tablet says. The nurse turns over to me and grabs my hand. I pull it back and shake my head vigorously. The nurse rolls her eyes and grabs the tablet out of the air. She places her thumb on the tablet and scans it. "Esmeralda, age 27, height six-foot-tall, weight 170 pounds, relatives unknown." The tablet spouts out random information.

I blink at her, completely at a loss for words.

She then faces the tablet back at me. "There's nothing to fear," she says most condescendingly.

Begrudgingly, I held out my thumb for it to scan. He then spouts out my information. "Elena Sandoval, age 12, birthday January 25th, height is five feet and three inches, father Ernesto Sandoval, mother Sylvia Sandoval, relative Maxine Sandoval." He then pauses for a moment and scans my entire body. "Facial recognition complete, menstruation cycle pending…" There was another pause, but this one felt longer. "Estimation within 5-12 weeks." My eyes completely widen, and I shake my head vigorously once again. I felt violated by the amount of information they have.

I could almost hear my father say from the back of my mind, "Knowledge is power. If you give away your information, may god forbid they use it against you."

Cedric the hologram finally pops up and takes a bow before shutting off.

The nurse begins to pack up her items and looks back into my eyes. "Any questions?"

I clutch my fist at my sides, trying not to attack the nurse. "Where is he? You promised you'd tell me where he is!"

My voice cracks just a little.

I hate this. It's their fault. It's the G.C.P.O.A.'s fault that I'm here without my parents.

Esmeralda rolls her eyes and takes my hand while the other is on the cart. When we reach the door, she looks into where the peephole should be. At her command, the door opens, and next to it is a man wearing the same red and black uniform the G.C.P.O.A. had on. She flirtatiously shoves me to the officer and in a sweet voice she says, "Take her to the cafeteria, will you officer?"

I could've sworn I almost puked in my mouth.

"Certainly." He winks at her and grabs my wrist. I turned back to give her one last glance, but by then she was already on her way down the hall.

Great. Leave me with my enemy. Attempting to glare at the officer, I motion my head in his direction, which he turns away. He simply stares ahead of the hallway, avoiding any eye contact.

4

I am completely lost.

This place is a huge labyrinth judging by the multiple twists and turns, well precisely five lefts and six rights, but even with that information, I would still be lost by the number of hallways there are. Not to mention, all the halls looked the same despite each door having a different color of tape stuck to it. I assumed they coordinated with the colors of our prison uniforms, as some were the shade of blue, purple, pink, and green. From the outside, they looked like normal white doors until an officer stepped next to a door with their holotablet. The door would open sideways, revealing its metal interior. I'm not sure who they are trying to fool, but it wasn't me anymore. Nothing about this was normal.

There would be moments when my officer needed to pull out a map just to see where we were. He would mutter a curse word and make another turn. I tried to look over his shoulder to see, but of course, he wouldn't let me catch a glimpse.

"It's confidential." He says, jerking the device further from my field of vision.

I rolled my eyes and continued to slouch against the wall until he was ready to lead me to where we were supposed to go. After walking for what felt like three miles, we finally came to a stop in front of an elevator. There were at least four other kids dressed in similar outfits as mine, with the exception that they wore different colors. Each one was escorted by their officer.

"Floor 109," my officer snaps. It didn't take long until we reached my floor, but before we did, one child, in particular, came in with chains on his hands and feet. He appeared to be around the age of fifteen, or maybe older. "Hurry up," snaps the officer next to him. Everyone shared glances of fear but merely stayed quiet until we arrived at our floor.

A few more steps later, right in front of me, were the large cafeteria doors completely wide open. I was in awe of the number of kids that were in there, along with the holy grail of food that was lined up. For a second, a split second, I almost forgot that I was a prisoner until I heard my brother's voice. From the farthest side of the cafeteria, he meets my eyes. He drops his food and sprints right toward me. He was wearing an outfit like mine except that his outfit was purple instead of blue.

He looked completely restless.

"Max!" I yell and embrace him in my arms. "Are you okay? Did they do anything to you?" I scanned his eyes, searching for any answers he could give me, but all I saw was sorrow. He proceeds to press his head into my chest as his arms tighten around me.

"I thought you were dead! I saw you in the room…El, you wouldn't wake up! You wouldn't wake up El, and they won't tell me where mom is!" he speaks in Spanish to me while hyperventilating. "Por favor, no me dejes solo," he whimpers.

He's been so scared, and I couldn't have been there. Dammit. If only I had woken up sooner.

"Max, it's going to be okay," I whisper into his ears. "Dad must be back from his trip right now, he'll protect mom. He'll save us."

He only shakes his head in defeat. Even I knew escape would be impossible. Who knows when we'll be back home.

"Alright, break it up, you two." An officer behind Max grabs him and rips him out of my grasp like a rag doll.

I felt my heart drop and bleed. What I was about to do made me appear as desperate as my mother. *Is this how she felt when we were taken away?*

"No!" I yell in desperation, positioning myself between them. "He's my brother!" I kick him where the sun does not shine and pull my brother away. Everyone was staring at us and gasped at what I did, both out of curiosity and fear.

His officer quickly gets up and punches me across the face. My cheek stung whilst I fell to the ground.

"Elena." My brother shrieks as he is pulled by other officers.

So close. He was just an arm's width away from me.

This all felt like déjà vu, except I was the one fighting. Before I get to my feet, my officer holds me down. "You'll see him after the day is over. Come on." He pulls me away from them.

"Max!" I give one great yelp before I am taken out of the cafeteria.

"Elena!" he screams back while wrestling the officer, but it is no use. He was too small to fight back, and I was too weak to do anything. Everyone in the room stared at us, some shaking their heads in disappointment.

Some kids began to cry. They gave me a look of pity and resonated with equal hopelessness.

I glance up at the officer, who is now pressing me against the wall. His eyes finally met my gaze. There was a small scar close to his cheek next to his brown eye, while the other eye was grey. They were completely captivating as if they showed two different sides of the same coin. His face was a little scruffy, almost as if he just woke up and didn't have time to shave. He reminded me of those funny army figures my brother had. His face is strong and very angular, just like the rest of the other officers, and might've been about two or three times taller than me. Like those toy army soldiers, he looked like he had come back from the war by the looks of the bags under his bloodshot eyes.

Yikes! This man must've taken a long night shift.

"You idiot." He pushes me harder against the wall. A small gleam of light hits my eye at that exact moment. I look down and notice his name tag spelling out Charles. "Listen to me." He presses me harder against the wall. My eyes once again lifted to meet his. "You will see your brother later but, in the meantime, I will be taking you with kids your age. You will spend the day doing whatever they say, and I will be in charge of patrolling you." The words coming out of his mouth sounded less harsh than I thought. They had a specific inflection in his voice, like a father yelling at his daughter rather than a sergeant yelling at his cadets.

"Do you understand?" He shoves me one more time, which takes the air out of my lungs. "Yes sir," I said in my most fierce voice, though, to Charles, it might as well come out as a whisper.

Once those words escape my mouth, he finally releases me, turns away, and walks straight ahead. For a moment, I stood there wheezing and clutching my chest with one hand and my head with the other. Somehow, I managed to catch up to him on time as we went back to the elevators. When we get back on, he presses the '110' button and the same process happens all over again.

This floor felt a little different from the others. I'm not sure if my eyes were deceiving me, but the hallways appeared to be narrower, and the doors had numbers on them. Some even had strange symbols.

By the time we got to a certain pair of double doors, we met at another cafeteria, except this one had people who were in my age range. A lot of them had the same baby blue color on their uniforms.

"Go eat." Charles orders without looking into my eyes. He shoves me forward with an iron toss, causing me to almost trip. I glare back at him and take a plate.

Looking at the table, I couldn't help but salivate at the number of choices there were. There was lobster, sushi, escargot, dumplings, tamales, crepes, pho, curry, and much more that I couldn't recognize. I glance over to my left shoulder and see three large doors, labeled Desserts, Breakfast, and Lunch (the one I came out of). The girl next to me smiles and abruptly cheers "The tacos here are to die for!" as she walks up to the man flipping tortillas. She orders two tacos al pastor and holds out her hand. "I'm Angela. Guess you're new here? You seemed pretty confused."

I gaze at her hand and back into her eyes. I make a small smile, admitting my confusion.

"Elena, but you may call me Ella or El for short." I shake her hand. Her eyes were the color of caramel and honey mixed together with a dash of lightheartedness. In comparison to mine, her skin was a few shades darker.

"I think I'll just stick with Ella," she giggles.

"I love your hair" I compliment her braids. They were extremely long and beautifully woven with green and blue that contrasted with her dark hair.

She gave me a sad smile before responding with, "Thanks, my father braided these before I was taken away."

Not really knowing what more to say, we both share an understanding nod and I order the same thing. We move over to the soda dispenser and fill our cups with our drinks. Once we have all we need, she grabs my hand and takes me into another pair of double doors.

Boy was it loud.

Imagine over two hundred kids talking at the same time, screaming, shouting, and pop music being blared. That is exactly what was happening.

The room was filled with benches and tables that spread around to the end. There were also levels of floors where other kids waved at us from above. If my mother was here, she would not want me anywhere above the 2nd level of this place due to her fear of heights and her overprotective nature. She tugs on my hand once more and leads me into a crystal glass elevator. We reach floor five and exit. Judging by my confusion, she adds "I want you to meet my friends," and jumps excitedly.

I just give a shaky thumbs up and continue to follow her.

"Don't worry, they don't bite, except for Xander, he might."

We pass through a series of benches until we finally meet the gang. On the corner of the table was a girl with blonde hair, who appeared to be sleeping. Next to her was a boy wearing glasses who was picking at his food. Right in front of those two was the scary boy from earlier. Only this time, he was chained to the table and his officer was nowhere in sight. None of the officers were. Strange.

She slides right next to him and bumps his shoulder. He looks up at me analyzing my every movement and rolls his eyes. "Seriously Angela. Did you befriend a newbie? Couldn't you have recruited anyone else?"

"Yes, Xander, a newbie. She could be of some use to us." She pats the space next to her, gesturing for me to sit. I take a seat, trying to hide my uneasiness. *Guess she was not kidding about Xander.*

"Everyone, I would like you to meet Ella," she announces to the group. None of them bothered to look me in the eye since the other guy was picking at the food and the girl with blonde hair remained still.

Disappointed by their responses, Angela instead tells me about them. The boy in chains is Xander who she claims 'is not that bad once you get to know him', but I have my suspicions. Did I mention that he is chained up to the table? If that doesn't send red flags, I don't know what will.

His uniform was a dark navy blue instead of a baby blue like the rest of us. He was at least 4 inches taller than me, which made him appear even more intimidating. His skin was very pale, almost translucent. He had a buzz cut and was covered with bruises from head to toe. In front of us was Kim. His actual name followed the lines of Min-Lee Kim, but he was very insistent we call him Kim. He had wavy dark hair that appeared to be very smooth and looked about the same age as all of us, except for Xander.

"Kim is what my sister used to call me." he would explain as he finally started to eat his food after picking at it. "Kim likes to look at his food. He thinks that they put something in it but so far, he's found nothing." Angela explains to me.

Maybe Kim was on to something.

I stare at the food in front of me and take a bite. There was nothing unusual about it. In fact, I would say that these tacos are pretty good but not as good as the ones my father made in the backyard on the weekends. I remember how nice the sun shone above us, where the grass appeared to be greener, and all the clouds would disappear out of sight. It was a perfect day to rest on the hammock right under the fig tree we grew. In the background, there would be Spanish music blaring on the side while my mother danced. My father would stop and watch her for a while before he joined her.

"Ella. Earth to Ella!" Angela waves her hand in front of my eyes.

"Huh, maybe there is something in this food," Xander adds bitterly. I come out of my thoughts and stare at the girl sleeping in front of me. "Sorry, I was just thinking of something." I shake my head and make eye contact.

"You're thinking of them. Aren't you?" Kim looks away from all of us and down at the people below. He pauses for a moment, almost as if he was also thinking back to when they took him away. "It's sick that they built this system all because they want our parents to work more," Kim adds bitterly and turns back to the three of us and gives one slight glance at the blonde girl.

Before I could respond, the pop music above us stopped and was replaced by a woman's voice. Angela taps the girl in front of us a few times until she finally wakes up with a startle. From one side of her cheek to the other, I notice she has freckles. Her eyes were brown, just like the rest of us. She glances around and makes a hand gesture to Angela with a smile on her face.

Angela points at me and uses hand signals. Recognizing a few of them, it occurred to me that she was using sign language.

A voice in the speaker then brings my attention once again. "Hello everyone, please pick up your plates and resume your schedule with your fellow *companions*." The woman chirps. An alarm then followed, causing all the children below to panic.

Companions?

From the bottom floor, officers came out from the double doors holding a GPS mechanism. They each walked around until each one of them found their child. Others tried to open the doors to run, but all of them had been locked. From the elevator, I spot Charles and he spots me. When the officers arrive at the table, I notice one of them holding what appears to be a leash. Turns out that the leash was for Xander. Angela gives Xander a sympathetic look as she is moved aside. While his officer puts on a collar around Xander's neck, the rest of our officers grab us by the arms and guide us outside of the cafeteria. From the corner of my eyes, I can see some kids still struggling to escape from their 'companions' and, in return, got beaten with a makeshift baton.

When Charles and I reach the hallways again, he lets my arm go like some kind of slinky. I grimace and shoot him a glare.

"Ouch! That hurt my arm!" I exclaim.

He ignores my complaint, and peers down at his phone, squinting his eyes at the bright screen. I not so sneakily go on my tippy toes and catch a glimpse of the corner. To my bewilderment, I saw a photo of myself. There I was, looking half-conscious. I was lying on a medical bed with my left arm bleeding through the bandages and with wires and machines all around me. I must've gotten a bad concussion because the top of my head was wrapped as well.

Oh god, I looked awful.

I couldn't imagine what Max's reaction was when he saw me like this.

He notices me peering over the screen and shuts the device immediately. "Where are we heading to?" I question him.

He continues to stare straight, avoiding my gaze completely. He doesn't answer me for a while until we finally reach another pair of double doors. "Class."

In front of us stood a line of kids wearing different colored outfits. Some were wearing shades of blue, and others had pink. I glanced at their shoes and saw that they too were also wearing black ankle bands.

That must be how they've been tracking us. I noted.

If I were to escape, I would need to get these things off Max and me. The real question is, how would I do that without getting electrocuted? Not to mention how on earth am I going to get us to pass our 'companions' on the way out and escape out of the building without getting lost or trapped? Where on earth would we go even if we did escape? Where would we hide? What would they do to us if we got caught?

My mind instantly listed off different scenarios, each one scarier than the next. I can only imagine what it is like to escape outside of here, and better yet, survive after getting caught.

When it was time, each of us went inside one by one without our officers by our side. I quickly stepped forward and took an available seat. There were at least forty seats in total, all equally spaced and facing the board. There was only one seat left in the back, and that was for Xander.

By how his officer was dragging him, it made sense why he took so long. It was an effort for the officer to get Xander to the doorway as they both kept wrestling back and forth. I wasn't gonna lie, it was scary seeing him struggling, and even more so when the officer grabbed a taser from his pocket.

If you ask me, the companion seemed a little too excited to use the tool.

He kept on tasing Xander over and over, even though Xander finally seemed to be calming down. Everyone in the room looked shocked, no pun intended, except for the woman who was impatiently tapping her foot.

She stood there the whole time and didn't bother to intervene to help Xander catch his breath. Occasionally, she would stare at her elongated nails, examining their sharpness, and lean against the desk. She was probably waiting for the class to calm down so she could start. Sadly, it didn't take long for Xander to pass out on the floor with his hands still bound together. Xander's companion then glances at the teacher. She rolls her eyes and speaks with a Jersey accent. "Just do what you did last time. Chain the boy to the seat and leave." The companion nods and does exactly as he was told.

My eyes couldn't leave Xander's unconscious body.

"Hello everyone!" the teacher says, breaking the silence. "For those who have been recently added, welcome."

The teacher then moves to the front of the class, pressing her small wristwatch that activates several holograms. They soar through the air and land in front of each student displaying a cheerful Cedric.

"High five!" he chirped, raising his hand.

I tapped him with my finger, and like a strobe light, he'd flash on and off until a digital square was fully displayed at his side. He'd salute, tapping the tip of his hand to his outstretched forehead, and vanish. On the digital blue square, each person had their name and grade level right in front of them, including Xander who finally started breathing. Some looked impressed while others, who appeared to be older than me, who wore pink, looked ashamed. I glanced at my data and saw that I was enrolled as a 9th-grade level student when, in reality, I was just entering the 7th-grade.

After the holograms fade into the air, the small watch on the teacher's wrist levitates and starts scanning the classroom. Once it has finished, it then returns to its original place. That's when the teacher stood from her desk, facing the class, whispering "Perfect, a full class" and stared back at us.

"For those of you who have met me already, congratulations, our class is full, so this will be the last time you will be hearing this introduction." I hear people behind me sigh in relief. I found it funny when a kid in the corner muttered "finally" under his breath loud enough to hear.

The teacher glares and throws a whiteboard marker at him, silencing the class. "To those who are new, I am Ms. Charlotte. I will be your English teacher. You will do as I say, otherwise, you will be severely punished like Xander over here." She then gestures and tiptoes over him.

If it wasn't for the load of makeup she was wearing, I would've found her to be a little more intimidating. Her purple lipstick was as thick as it could be and smeared her teeth every time she sneered or smiled.

Her face, in simpler terms, looked like a cake that was covered in thick layers of frosting that had expired, which made her seem older than she was. Her eyebrows are more like two large caterpillars sitting on her face; they were quite bushy and wrongly glued on from the sides. What's worst of all is that I could almost feel the weight of her eyelashes judging by how heavy and clumpy they appeared every time she blinked. To top it all off, her hair was the color of a red fox's fur, except it was curly instead of straight, which made her look entirely like a clown.

"You are in this English class because of your writing and reading capabilities, whether that is a good thing or not." Ms. Charlotte states.

"Now, just because some of you are at this level of English doesn't mean that it correlates to your grade level. Some of you may have a 9th-grade level of English Composition, which is this class, but in actuality, you may be an 11th-grader. Hence, why your classes may differ."

She mutters something unpleasant under her breath pertaining to the older students who may have been held back.

The rest of the introduction was mainly going over material that I was too bored to pay attention to. I couldn't help but find myself dazed off in my imagination, most of the time wondering what I would have been doing at home. Those thoughts began to disappear with each new fresh worksheet handed to me.

By the time I had finished my fifth worksheet, Xander finally regained consciousness. When he realized that his companion was not in the room, his tense face relaxed a little. Just like that, the class was silent for a while until Ms. Charlotte gave us a small break, and by a small break, I mean a tantrum.

This woman completely snapped.

Every time the boy with the jokes spoke, she would throw something at him and yell at him to be quiet. When she had enough, she grabbed the kid who was muttering jokes under his breath and started to hit him with a ruler.

"I warned you all!" she yells and smacks him again. "This is what happens! Do not test me like Mason here! There will be consequences!" With every word she spoke, came another swing. Each hit became sturdier and harder until the ruler finally broke into pieces.

That's when she pulls another one behind her desk and proceeds to do the same thing just before Mason can run to the door. The boy next to me covers his ears and closes his eyes, afraid to see what is happening in the back corner of the classroom. I did the same, trying not to look behind me as best as I could, but that only sparked my curiosity. I take a glance at Xander only to see him covering his ears and looking straight ahead. He then turns his head and faces me.

For a brief moment, I understood what that gaze meant. *This is how it is. This is our cruel world.*

Hesitantly, my eyes shift to Mason's poor body. His back was completely drenched in blood and marks of the ruler. He was breathing quite heavily, and his salmon-pink clothes did not help with hiding the stains. Once she is done with him, she grabs her watch and presses a small button displaying a hologram. "We need a nurse," she angrily says to it.

After a few minutes pass, a nurse enters the classroom with the same outfit Esmeralda wore, and the rest of us get escorted out by our companions. I tried my best to avert my eyes from Mason and simply stare at the bear displayed on the nurse's hat as we were leaving, but once again, my eyes betrayed me. I quickly gave a glance that I knew I would regret. His back was a mess. Judging from the sight, something tells me that this was not his first time. There were far too many re-opened scars and bruises. They were all fresh as meat from a slaughterhouse.

If Ms. Charlotte could do this to us, what about the rest of us? I shudder at the possibilities, gripping my shoulders. These people aren't caretakers. They're predators. We might as well be zoo animals to them. They think they're helping, but really, all that we want is to be set free from our cages.

By the time the nurse finishes patching up his back, I exit the classroom with a chill down my spine.

# 6

In a long line, we all walked alongside our companions to the next destination, the gymnasium. The ones wearing pink departed in a different direction, while those of us who wore shades of blue entered one by one.

By the time I stepped into the gym, a blast of cold air coated my skin, leaving me shaking. I followed the boy in front of me where each line of kids was seated against rows and rows of bleachers that were close to being filled. As I walk up the stairs, a hand snatches my left arm and pulls me down next to them. I wince in pain, doing what I can to stop myself from screaming. I kick at them with my foot, and they release me.

"I am so sorry, Ella!" the handler apologizes.

I find myself seated next to Angela, Xander, Kim, and the girl with blonde hair. "We were calling your name, but you didn't seem to hear us," Kim explains on behalf of Angela.

She gives me an apologetic look that I briskly wave off. My irritability was my personal downfall as it set me off in a bad mood. I tried to reassure her by saying "It's fine," but it came off as passive-aggressive. On the bright side, at least I wasn't bleeding. If I were, Angela might've gotten more than a kick from me. I can assure you of that. Heated and hot-headed, I take a few deep breaths to cool off. When I was ready, I traded seats with Kim and sat next to Angela to make her feel better. Everyone was already seated in the stands, waiting for something to happen. The lights dim and a spotlight lands directly at the center of the gymnasium.

"For those of you who know the drill, explain to the newbies." A small angry man yells into the microphone. From our distance, he looked like a small troll with an orange beard. I guessed he was the gym teacher based on the oversized tracksuit that failed to cover his hairy belly. Like Ms. Charlotte, he clicks the small device on his wrist and starts scanning us with holograms. They displayed the same information as before, except for the added data on our speed and strengths.

"That guy over there is coach Mike. Every day he does a rotation of exercises we must do," Angela explains to me as fast as possible. Her voice raced with her words as if she was running out of air to breathe.

Kim intervenes with a frown on his face. "Yesterday was basketball and today is dodgeball day.

When he blows the whistle, I need you to-" The coach
cuts him off by blowing the whistle that hangs outside the
pocket of his sweats.

"DUCK!" Xander yells, pulling the blonde girl
with him. Simultaneously, everyone covered their heads
with their hands and tucked themselves in between their
legs. Thousands of dodgeballs fell from the ceiling,
aiming right toward us. Some of us were screaming and
others were hit so hard that they were knocked out
breathless. When it finally ended, there was a loud sigh of
relief circling the bleachers. A silence was shared among
the crowds to see if our comrades were okay, thankfully
no nurses were needed and those who went unconscious
seemed to be waking up. I was hit a few times, but it was
nothing serious. All the impact went to my back.

As baffling as it is, gym teacher Mike was
laughing so ruthlessly that he was clutching his stomach
as if the attack of the dodgeballs was all nothing but a
laughing matter to him. After gathering himself for a
moment, he splits the gymnasium into two opposing
sides. The left and the right side. He conspicuously
observes the two sides and slides a bill out of his wallet.
He gestures the bill to someone standing outside of the

gymnasium and lets the companion take it from him, shaking their hands.

Unbelievable. Is this man child really going to bet on which side will win?

He pulls out his whistle and blows on it the second time. "Dodgeball time!" he barks, gesturing at us to move faster to the ground floor with dodgeballs at our sides. "I want both sides to show no mercy. If my betted team doesn't win, I'll have you all run laps tomorrow! Come on! Keep moving! I'm looking at you, Wellie."

"It's William!" the boy corrects, shooting daggers at the coach.

As we line the balls up in the center of the gym, the coach blows his whistle for the last time. That's when all hell broke loose.

They were flying all over the place. Blurs of yellow, green, blue, and red clouded my vision as they flew past my head, flying like saucers. I ran to the back, where I witnessed the mayhem.

"Movie it!"

"Ouch!"

"Hey, you can't do that!"

The best way I can describe it is that they went from human beings to monsters within seconds. The ball became their weapon, and the gymnasium was a battlefield. At that point, it didn't matter if a friend got hurt or broke a nose in the process. What mattered was the satisfaction of being victorious (or in this case, not running laps). The catch was, we didn't exactly know what side Coach placed his bet on. It was a fifty-fifty percent chance.

Plunk!

At the bottom of my foot was a bright yellow ball that had hit the boy in front of me when he tried to catch it with his arms. I snatch the ball with great hope and use it as a shield in the middle of an armorless battlefield. With my free hand, I seized a few dodgeballs and started to aim at those who had a blind spot. It saved me several times from getting hit all around until I found myself face to face with a girl with blue hair that was slowly faded into a murky green. As we made eye contact, her blood-red acrylic nails gripped the bright ball tightly.

I'm done for.

A smirk followed upon her almond-shaped face as though she had read my mind. I held up my ball to block myself, but it was already too late. She moved in the blink of an eye and threw the ball at me with all her might.

Thud!

"You're out!" Mike yells as I lay on the floor with my hands covering my eyes. I could've sworn that I had broken something by the way the rubber ball collided with the bridge of my nose, but thankfully, it didn't.

I was told to head to the back to mope around with those who were also out of the game. The acoustics were just as noisy. From behind the bleachers, I spotted the blonde-haired girl and sat by her side. A kid the same age as us was talking to her (well, trying to communicate with her) by holding up a tooth still covered in blood, and making hand gestures to demonstrate what happened to him.

Apparently, he was lost in the crowd, and out of nowhere, a ball flew straight at his face, taking out a tooth, and thus he pulled out an ice pack that a nurse had given him. The blonde girl's face scrunched up in almost disgust when she saw the bloody tooth held right in front of her eyes. She then gave the boy a sympathetic look as he started to stand up.

He gives her a sincere smile, revealing a gap in the front of his teeth where it had once laid. He then walks to one of his friends, explaining the whole story again. They give him pats on the back, leaving me alone next to the girl with blonde hair. We sat there waiting for the game to end, or at least for Xander, Kim, or Angela to come to the back of the gymnasium, where all the 'losers' were located. Despite kids screaming, running, and talking throughout, the silence between the blonde girl and me was killing me.

What should I say? Should I wave? Does she remember me from lunch?

"There you are!" Kim exclaims, brightening his gaze at the recognition of the blond girl. He sits right at her side and breaks the silence between us, properly introducing me to Catherine, who was just as relieved as I was to break the tension. Luckily, I knew at least the alphabet to introduce myself officially to her.

In response, she gave me a small smile. We both had one thing in common: nicknames. She preferred to be called Cat, the same way I preferred to be called El or Ella. Though, mostly it is Max and my parents who call me El. Ella was mainly a name my old friends liked to call me because it sounded pretty and rolled off the tongue better. During our exchange, there would be times when she would speak to me instead of using sign language or tap the floor in Morse code.

Everyone in Crinx United was obligated to learn it, just in case a war broke out with the opposing country, called Laster. We had a war with the country over two decades ago, but it lasted for quite a long time. Our latest treaty has held up thus far, but every now and then my family saw headlines of a potential nuclear attack. In my opinion, I think they should've taught sign language in conjunction with the mandatory Morse code.

Granted, there are plenty of things I think our government should've done. My most prominent one is the eradication of the G.C.P.O.A. and the taking of children. Who on earth thought it was a good idea to separate us from our families so that our parents could work like machines? It's utter insanity.

In response to keeping the conversation going, I asked her about her family. The second those words left my mouth, I immediately regretted asking. She became teary-eyed and closed off.

"Who knows? They took me away before I was able to see my grandparents after school…I hope they're doing well." She gives a final pause and turns her frown into a smile. Like any kid here, I knew the pain was still there.

Kim decides to speak up but gets interrupted by the whistle. "Alright, game time is over, you wusses. Right-wing wins! Get to your next class!" Those on the right cheered while those on the left mumbled very unpleasant words.

From the corner of my eye, I spotted Xander and Angela cheering with hands in the air, which was a response that was expected from Angela but never from Xander. He seemed almost human until his eyes spotted someone far in the distance. That's when his face turned sour once more. My eyes follow his gaze only to realize his companion is there with his chains and leashes ready at his side. He waves them in front of his face, taunting Xander from the opposite side of the room.

What an as-

"Come on." Charles snaps, ushering me out of the gym.

Thankfully, he kept his distance and didn't bother to grab my hand like the others. He instead made a stop at the medical center where my shoulder had been examined after the game. Across from us was the kid whose tooth had been knocked out. He was given a new ice pack, which made his companion roll her eyes and give him a scolding. Some children who were diabetic had come to restock on insulin, and others traded their glasses for cases of contacts.

BEEP!

BEEP!

BEEP!

The lights flash red, causing all the nurses to stop at their stations.

"More of them?" grumbles the nurse over the alarm. She speedily changes the bandages and scurries to her cart. Within seconds, children, both old and young, came rolling in a similar state to what I was in when I had first arrived. They had their regular clothes on and were soon to be met by another crew of nurses. It was all too gruesome to see. A boy passing by barely had his eyes open and appeared to have bullet wounds on both legs. A girl younger than Max was rushed in with a nurse yelling "Second-degree burns".

The poor girl had her arm burned badly enough to fill the room with the scent of burnt flesh. A pain of regret shoots right through me, reminding me of the sight Max had to see when they had to wheel me in. Thankfully, I did not find Max here and I hope I never need to. I don't know what I would do with myself if he ever got hurt, and I wasn't there to support him. Nor did I want to consider the possibility of losing him.

After being rushed out of the medical center, I was sent to two other classes, Chemistry and History. Each one was more daunting than the other. Kim and Cat made it a bit less boresome, as they were my lab partners in my chemistry class. The gist of the two classes was that we learned about filtration in chemistry and were fed loads of propaganda in the other class. The teacher played a bunch of videos featuring Cedric, who explained the importance of having our parents work day and night in our modern-day economy. A large sum of their paychecks was going to be used to fund the military to 'protect' us. Then, in the end, Cedric encourages the upperclassmen to apply to be next year's new sector of G.C.P.O.A. officers.

It angered me.

When classes were done, I was finally led to the cafeteria, where many families were united. Correction, families, as in everyone else other than adults and parents. Many siblings, cousins, and friends huddled up in groups, some laughing and others crying in each other's arms. I noticed a handful of us didn't have any loved ones to run to.

"I haven't been able to find him." Cried a girl in pink.

"Chin up, Melissa, maybe he's somewhere else. He's safe."

"How do you know that? What if in another facility, he's in danger?"

"Your nephew will be fine." He reassures her.

Mid-step, a hand captures my arm. To my relief, it was Max alongside a little girl in pigtails wearing the color green. On her head were a pair of bright yellow headphones. He tugs on my arms just a little to pull me into a small hug. When we pull away, I see a small tear he attempts to hide as he gestures to the little girl to come closer. She shyly scoots next to Max, grabbing his left arm and putting some distance while I'm on my brother's right-hand side. Her eyes avoid my gaze as she stares at the floor. In response, my brother squeezes her hand and introduces me to her while we head to the fruit bar to eat. "It's okay Mika, this is my sister, Elena," he said in a small voice.

"But she prefers El because apparently, Elena is too long. Don't worry, she's nice. Well, sometimes." He jokes as I roll my eyes.

Says the boy whose name is Maxine, but prefers Max.

"Hello, Mika." I give her a small, subtle smile.

She blushes and points at the food with her other hand, rubbing her tummy.

"Good idea let's ditch the fruits for now," Max says as he holds her hand, guiding her past the crowd and onto the plate station. With one hand I grab a plate for myself and with my free hand I reach it out for Mika to shake. At first, she was hesitant and a little fearful at the sight. I gave her a nod of assurance and slowly move my arm away. In response, she quickly changes her mind and shakes my hand firmly. My brother smiles in approval as we make our way to the rows and rows of berries and exotic fruits. Mika's eyes glimmered like gold once she spotted a strawberry tart in the dessert section.

After settling down and going through plates and bowls of food and filling out our mouths and stomachs to their uttermost desires, Max and Mika begin to talk and laugh. It gave me some relief knowing that Max had somewhat of a good time and made a friend while we were here.

Friends.

I wonder if my best friend Kelly is here, or John, or Lia. It's too late to think of them now. They were probably in a different facility, given that they were one of the first to be taken. All I can do is stick with the people I met today.

Wait a minute.

Where are Angela, Kim, Cat, and Xander? I hope they aren't in trouble. Especially Xander. I spun around to see if I could locate any of them. I was surprised when more blue's came in and none of the kids were them.

"Who are you looking for?" Max asks worriedly. He was very good at detecting my emotions.

"No one. I was simply seeing if they had any figs, like the ones back home." I reply, avoiding causing any tension that might flatten his contempt. He was happy enough to have Mika and me. I can find my friends later.

"Oh. I didn't see them either." He follows Mika out of the table and the two search the bundles of fruits that are in the cafeteria. He comes back with a small orange instead.

"Thank you, Max." I smile. He returns the gesture and I take in the moment. His little smile. It's been a while.

When dinner was over, our companions came in, rushing to collect us. It happened quickly enough for them to snatch up the little ones in purple without alarming them. When Mika sensed them, she briskly grabbed hold of my leg, but eventually was pulled away from us and to the claws of her companion. She hit him in the arm and fought like hell to stay with Max and me.

She can put up a fight, that's for sure.

Once she is forced away, Max and I are escorted out by our companions. At that moment, the slightest fear of being separated again surfaced in my thoughts.

Physically separating the two of us, Max's companion grabs his arm and guides him along the same route Charles and I were walking to. When we finally reached the same door, those thoughts disappeared.

"We'll pick you up in the morning." Both companions say simultaneously before closing the doors. Alone, there was a strange pause between Max and I. It was almost as if we didn't know what to say when there was so much that had happened.

"Max-"

"I am glad you're awake, Ella," he abruptly says. "I was this close to drawing a mustache on your face if you didn't wake up." He holds up his hand with his fingers close to touching. *A classic thing Max would say, of course.*

I roll my eyes and make a face. "Real mature of you, Max. I'll remember that when you pass out." I give him a jokingly glare and lightly punch his shoulder. He chuckles, feeling assured, and runs into his room, probably to read another comic book or play with a device. Meanwhile, I turn on the TV to keep my mind at bay. At first, nothing appeared on the screen. It flickered on and off until a news channel began to play. It was very static, and the person filming appeared to be in the middle of a protest. The screen glows clear, showing people shouting and holding posters saying "GIVE US BACK OUR CHILDREN" in unison. Some posters had an image that I've seen in the media before. It was an image of two elephants and a baby elephant.

"The Homing Herd," I say out loud. A memory flashes in my mind.

"When in doubt, listen to what's around you. Never go alone and trust no one." Dad said before he left for his work.

He was one of those people who believed that there were secret groups who helped kids get back home after being captured. A common symbol they had was two big elephants with a baby elephant. It was rumored that they hid underground or in the sewers. Mom was a firm believer as well. She would always tell me to come to the TV whenever the media talked about "The Homing Herd". When I first saw it on the TV with my mom, it showed a billboard displaying the name and the image. It was almost as if the organization was saying "We're here and we are coming".

Now it is even more evident that "The Homing Herd" may be true and not a rumor.

The camera pans out to law enforcement buildings that were sprayed, painted, and burning. They all had two elephants and a baby elephant on them. Parents all around were full of anger, some holding firearms and others holding shields. They all made elephant noises as if that was their roar and walked forward to the other side of the street.

In the corner, something catches the camera's eye as it pans out once again to a G.C.P.O.A. officer pinning down a pregnant mother to the ground. His hands were grasping her sides, and her dress was stained with dirt and ashes. With her hands, she holds her stomach, shrieking in horror. In defense, a swarm of people begins to attack the officer and aid the woman.

Horrified, I pressed the remote, attempting to change the channel. 'What the heck!" I yell as it does nothing to change the scenery. "I can't have Max seeing this." The language switched with each click.

It wasn't going away.

Before I decided to turn it off, the channel changed back to English with the camera panning over to a battered citizen. He resembled someone I knew but couldn't recall the name.

"Look at what they've done!" The man angrily shouts to the camera. Bruises contoured his cheeks and his left hand held something of what appeared to be a briefcase. "You see all of this? All of this because of selfish greed!!!"

Mr. Dillion. He was our school principal.

"OUR CHILDREN! OUR POOR CHILDREN!" various voices erupted over him. They cover the camera with their poster signs and bring havoc to a specific area they are standing in front of.

What on earth is going on?

Out of nowhere, someone from the crowd throws a match and catches the government building on fire. Two planes simultaneously drop bombs overhead, leaving them to drop on the ground. The camera goes out and changes the image to a cartoon of a girl going on an adventure. She jumped around and squealed with joy, without a care in the world.

She is lucky. I envy her.

"You saw that too?" Max says in a hushed voice. In his left hand, he held a baseball. The scuff and dirt marks looked like the original one he had; the one our dad caught for him at a baseball game. It was a home run. I remember how happy Max was when he realized the baseball player had signed it after the game was over. It was legendary. After that came the rest of his baseball collection.

Which one was he holding last?

"Yeah, I did." I paused before continuing. "Don't worry Max. I'll figure something out." I walk up to him and touch his shoulder with one arm.

He looks up and flinches.

My shoulder. Mom. Dad. Home.

"I'm alright Max. Promise. Todo va a estar bien." I hold up my pinky, assuring him as best as I can.

He gives me a faint smile and disregards my pinkie. I crouch close to him, proving the truth in my words.

"Mira Maxine, necesito que seas fuerte mientras estamos aquí. It won't be easy, but I will find a way for us to get out of here. I just need you to be patient." Behind us, the television goes static, but nothing appears.

"Okay?" I raise my voice and stare into his eyes as my father would.

"Okay," he mumbles under his breath.

"Good. I pinkie promise we'll be alright."

"I pinkie promise we'll be alright." He repeats after me. We both release and click our fingers, just like we used to. However, our previous promises were more achievable.

"Good. I'll be going to sleep now. Don't stay up too late and remember to brush your teeth." I yawn exaggeratedly.

He dolefully waves me off as I head into the restroom closest to my room. When the door closes behind me, my shoulders unclench. The restroom lights hang over me like curtains, caressing my face as I stand in front of the mirror. My left arm sagged like it would after a vaccine and the baby blue outfit made my features look worse as it is. My dark wavy hair was loose and knotted, the bags under my eyes became a new addition, and bruises from today covered me from head to toe. I somehow seemed older and much more malnourished. Cheesy as it sounds, I couldn't believe that I was the girl staring back. She had the same face, hair, eyes, and look, yet something felt off. *Something has changed.*

This is not me.

This *was* not me.

Just unbelievable.

Now that I was alone, it all hit at once. I turned on the shower head to create some noise so that Max didn't need to worry. When the coast was clear, I leaned against the wall, facing away from the mirror, and sighed. I wanted to cry. I wanted to punch something. I wanted the door to burst open and have my parents come in. I wanted them to be here to tell me that this was all a bad dream. I wanted to scream until my voice was gone.

Everything just suddenly changed, and I couldn't do anything. We were so close. If only they hadn't checked the closet, we could've been watching TV, eating at the table, annoying each other, and doing all these normal things even if we couldn't go outside. Just the thought of our current situation made my hands shake. I grew unsteady by the second and crouched on the floor, staring at the cabinets in front of me. My breaths became uneasy and all I could do was cover my head with my hands. I was hyperventilating uncontrollably. It was an awful sensation, one I never dealt with prior to all of this.

"It's going to be okay… we'll escape and be safe at home." I tell myself over and over until I felt somewhat stable to where I was breathing normally. Slowly my hands loosened their grip on my hair and fell at my sides. I take a final deep breath and look up at the mirror, standing completely still. A single tear fell from my right eye and down to my cheek. Pools of water from both eyes threatened to pour, but I refused to let them. One tear was more than enough. Anymore more than that, the entire ocean would flood my land of peace.

I had to be strong. No, I *needed* to be strong. Strong for the both of us.

Get a grip, now is not the time.

In the background, past the sound of the shower, I hear Max murmuring some words and making sounds with his toys. It felt oddly normal to hear him playing, almost as if the sound grounded me more to myself.

When I turned back to the mirror, my smile collapsed to a thin line. If Mom saw what I looked like right now, she would compare me to one of her patients from her work at the nursery home, specifically her patient, Grouchy Georgie. She would make jokes and go on and on about her day at work while preparing something for me to eat as a way to comfort me. Meanwhile, Dad would've probably been freaking out and questioning me about what was wrong. Even now, I wonder what they are doing.

Dad was definitely home by now after his business trip. He was scared we'd be gone by the time he was back, but my mother convinced him to go since we needed the money after she quit her job to take care of us. I can only imagine his reaction coming home.

Max and I were gone, like every other neighbor's child.

"We'll escape. We'll go home, and everything will be okay." I repeat as if it were to be a prayer.

I grab my toothbrush and toothpaste and start brushing, yet still staring at the girl in front of me. Like the water flowing from the shower head, all of this began to sway me away. The strokes of the yellow toothbrush felt liberating as the minty scent coated my mouth.

A sense of cleanliness is just what I needed.

I run my hands under the cool water, baptizing my face, hoping for myself to wake up like it was all a dream. I looked up and started over until it was evident that nothing was going to change except for my perception. Pieces of what resembled my father surfaced the further I tried to recollect myself. My brown eyes and tanned skin, along with parts of my facial features such as my rounded nose, reminded me of my father. Most of the features of my mother had gone to Max. The resemblance of our faces is all I have left of them now.

When I finished cleaning myself, I grabbed the hairbrush to take care of the curls in my hair. The memory of the officer grabbing my hair down flashes in my head as I put it up in a ponytail like I always do.

Like I always did, to be exact.

When I am done, I turn off the lights, leaving the silhouette of the girl behind me. "Good night, Max," I mumble, crashing into my bed. The weight of my body sinks into the covers like a bear in a cave. I was completely sore and exhausted from all that my body had undergone. As I was about to doze off, a small figure with cat-like eyes hovered over me.

"El, can I sleep with you tonight?" Max whispers. Normally, I would object to this, but I allowed it, all things considered.

"Did you brush your teeth?" I asked him.

"Yes," he replies, nodding his head. I recognized the baseball in his hand but didn't bother questioning it.

"Very well," I say as I move to the opposite side of the bed. The room was silent without the sounds of the crickets that usually came from my bedroom window. It made it unsettling and foreign. It took an endless amount of staring at the ceiling and envisioning myself back home to make myself slip away willingly. That is until Maxine.

"El, I'm scared." I heard him creep at my bedside, this time sounding half asleep. The weight of his words surfaces around me. I couldn't ignore them even if I tried.

"I know Max,"

I am too.

I turn my body to face him.

"It's going to be okay," I whisper back, petting the top of his head like a small cat. It's what my mother used to do whenever he was anxious. She did this on his first day of school, every single doctor's appointment, and at baseball games. Even now it seems to work because he then began to slowly fall asleep.

"Can you tell me a story?"

Usually, our dad would be the one to do this. He told us various stories consisting of adventure, duels, magical fights, and large kingdoms. He'd occasionally use Maxine's stuffed animals to visualize the epic sword fights.

"How about another night?" I yawn. I was far too tired to come up with anything.

"Tomorrow?"

"Maybe."

"Please."

"I promise you, one of these days, I'll tell you a bedtime story."

"Pinkie promise?"

"I pinkie promise." I curl my pinkie over his and snap our fingers as we pull away. For his sake, I half-heartedly hum a lullaby, hoping it is enough to keep his nightmares at bay. I waited until I was sure he had fallen into a deep slumber.

He shouldn't have to deal with this.

None of us do.

I was back at home.

Sweet. Sweet. Home.

With the greatest contempt a girl could ever have, I was sitting in the grass underneath the fig tree, gazing at the cloudless sky. In the background, familiar songs began to play, the ones my mother enjoyed the most. The blow of a baseball bat hitting against an object made me believe Max and my father were playing in the front yard. They were all tending to their daily duties while I lay in the grass basking everything in. A wave of cool air shifts the leaves of the fig tree ever so slightly that it blinds my eyes. When they realigned, the sky was no longer cloudless but rather covered in stars.

The only notion distracting me from the constellations was the slamming of doors and shrieks for help coming out of my neighbor's house. Alarmed, I lifted myself out of the grass and struggled to make my way inside as a strong wind blew me with great force, lifting me with each step I took. It was as if I were fighting a tornado. I pushed hard against the wind, but that only resulted in a scraped knee.

"Mami!" I yell out loud.

No response.

I take one more step, and the wind holds me down. It felt like there were invisible weights all over my body.

"Papi!" I call for my parents again as I reach the door with both of my hands.

No response.

Where are they?

BANG. A loud ring comes from my neighbor's house, followed by another shriek. Rapidly, I opened the door and inside stood a G.C.P.O.A. officer with a pistol in his hand. I covered my hand over my mouth, stopping myself from making a sound. His back was wide open for me to see.

No.

Blood covered the house from the kitchen tiles to the hanging lamps on our ceiling. Following the carnage, a powerful stench of his body odor stung in my nostrils. I held back the reflex to gag. As he stood there like a column, I noticed a small baseball with a familiar signature underneath his boot. He didn't appear to notice me but rather was focused on something hiding behind the couch. Quickly, I headed to the kitchen where the knives were. Closest to me glimmered a cleaver next to an uncooked steak. It was unstained and untarnished, unlike the rest of the living room.

Perfect.

I grabbed it confidently as I made my way to the living room. I wasn't sure where he went. I scanned the floors, searching for footprints. They scattered like rats and made their way around the room. The footprints were as big as my forearm and pronounced as the pool of blood it left behind. My heart sank when they led behind me.

"Boo." The officer whispers into my ear.

How did he find me?

I swung the cleaver quickly and ran back into the living room, not looking back at the fallen officer. In front of the couch was an image I wish I could unsee. This is where the blood was coming from…. all of them were covered with bullet wounds in places where I knew a person could not survive. The only one moving is my mother. She says something that I couldn't hear.

"What?" I say lightly as I hold her face close to mine.

"Wake up dearie." a familiar voice says, shaking everything near me.

Huh?

Everything became so fuzzy as though the world spun underneath my feet until all the images faded into a pitch-black space. "El!" My brother says, this time waking me up.

It was just a nightmare.

"I'm up. Stop Shaking me." I enunciate, brushing Max off. He sticks out his tongue and walks away, muttering about my laziness.

"Get showered and dressed," Esmeralda orders me. "You'll be heading to breakfast soon."

Yum, breakfast.

With that in mind, I did what she said.

Max was already gone with his companion by the time I had finished handling my business, showering, and changing. Meanwhile, Charles and Esmeralda flirted before it was time to lead me to the cafeteria. It's kind of freaky seeing how stoic they turned once they stopped talking and realized I was there.

Like last time, Charles did not talk to me nor bother to make any kind of conversation. It was almost like I wasn't there at all. When we got to the cafeteria, I was not going to lie, it was pretty disappointing. Every single kid needed to take a vitamin supplement to proceed past the doors. It was just like any gummy vitamin with the fruity taste of watermelon, which wasn't bad until I got to the aftertaste. Now that was awful.

I scurry in but am once again met with disappointment. Each of us needed to be seated to be given a plate of a prepped breakfast meal.

The mood of the room was dramatically different from yesterday. Instead of normal chatter, parts of the crowd became sounds of whispers. From what I can tell, they also must've seen last night's broadcast.

As I looked around for a seat, I noticed something, or more so, someone. From above, Angela was waving her arms gleefully and gesturing for me to come up to the same spot as before. When I got there and sat in my seat, a plate was handed to me. It consisted of a sliced waffle with strawberries on top, a fruit cup, eggs, two slices of sausages, and a glass of milk. Everyone seemed to have the same thing except for a few, which I assume has to do with dietary needs.

At first, it was only Angela, Xander, and I at the table. Xander was still in chains. I was tempted to ask why but didn't feel comfortable enough to do that just yet. They were talking among themselves about something they had been planning.

"Any recruits this time?" He asked her in a low enough voice for me to hear.

She shakes her head from side to side. "None, still trying to see if we have enough for this to work without being caught."

I raise my eyebrow at them while taking a bite from my plain waffle.

If only it came with some syrup instead of strawberries.

"You two do realize I am sitting here, right? I mean, I understand what you have is a secret, but I can hear you guys. Try to be a little more discrete next time." I say, not missing a beat on calling them out. "So, what are *we* talking about today?"

"Don't worry, I'll explain later," she tells me and thinks to herself this time.

"As long as you're not a snitch, that is," Xander adds while shooting a glance at Angela.

"I'm not."

Coming in came Kim and Cat, only this time Kim was no longer wearing glasses.

"You're not what?" Kim questions as he sits down.

"A snitch."

"You better not be. I may not look like much, but I can always kick your butt," Cat says with a smirk while posing her hands like a boxer.

The whole group then broke out into a laugh and resumed the conversation. Xander was quick to point out that Kim wasn't wearing his glasses. Kim explained that he felt annoyed with the glasses and went on a rant about his vision. Just like last time, he examined his food but did not find anything. Angela, on the other hand, insisted he investigate the vitamin gummy instead. We all agreed that the aftertaste was horrendous and was in deep need of an investigation. The only problem is that we would need to find a way to keep it in our mouth long enough to hide it or somehow sneak a second one unnoticed.

Just as we were brainstorming, a girl loudly screamed "Don't touch me!" at the level right below us. It was loud enough to hear past the speakers as people now began to stop and stare. We all looked over the railing to see what the commotion was about.

Turns out two insolent boys kept trying to grab a girl's hijab off her head.

"Stop it!" She would scream each time they tried. They each would say mean comments and words that struck a nerve within me.

There is one thing I hate more than the G.C.P.O.A., and that is bullies.

I grabbed a fruit cup and looked over at Cat, who was already out of her seat. She took Angela by the hand, but she was quick to sit back down. "Don't worry, you won't fight this time, it'll be me, and Ella," Cat tells Angela.

Angela pauses for a moment and reluctantly gets up, giving Cat a hesitant look.

"Save our seats?" Angela asks Xander and Kim. Immediately, they both nod.

"We'll be watching just in case you guys need help," Kim says.

"Trust me won't." Cat signs before we leave the table and head down to the level below us.

Since the place was crowded with kids my age, three things would happen if a fight were to break out:

Number one, not many will care or notice because everything is in disarray. They'll be too busy in their little bubbles to help or want to intervene. I call that the 'mind your own business' crowd.

Number two, there are people who do notice us but mainly watch for the sake of watching. They're the classic chismosos. I have been guilty of this a few times but during family gatherings.

Number three, some people have blood boiling and are ready to assess the situation. Here, an outside bystander will help us take their rear to the trash.

"She said stop!" Angela steps in next to the girl while Cat is in between them. Her arms were crossed, and her facial expression became serious. I was only about five steps away from them all.

"Oh please. She's fine." The boy puts his hands inside the pockets of the baby blue pants. He makes a subtle hand gesture that signals his friend to come forward.

The second boy speaks up and rolls his eyes so far back to his head. "We're just having a bit of fun." Both boys were brunettes. Boy number one was shorter than boy number two. They seemed like they were twins or, if possible, cousins. The shorter boy went as far as telling the girl with the hijab to play along with them while the taller one tried to shoo us away, which led me to move closer.

I stood behind boy number two with my arms crossed like Cat. "Uh-huh, you both have some severe issues if you can't understand what "no" and "stop" mean.

She clearly is not having fun and doesn't want anything to do with you two." I shoot a dirty look at boy number two, who seemed off-put by my gesture but hid his emotions by walking closer to boy number one. That seemed to give him confidence. With them, it felt as if everything went into one ear and out to the other.

These two were not going to stop.

Angela understood this as well and attempted to ease the situation.

"Look, unlike you two, I'm a lover, not a fighter," Angela says calmly. One of them scoffs but doesn't say anything. Instead, the shorter one turns the tables and verbally tries to intimidate Angela. It was almost as if they were trying to spark her fire and get us all even madder. Instead, she shakes her head and tries to rush the girl away from them. As she talks to the girl, I slowly move in between them, just in case something goes wrong.

Proving my point, boy number one steps forward and reaches his hand out to grab the girl's hijab once again. Everything suddenly spun into slow motion. Quickly, I step in grabbing his hand mid-air, and spinning him around like a ballerina. Disorientated, he moves away from me but resumes to come at me full speed.

"Lucky for you two I grew up as a fighter," I smirk and push the fruit cup up his nose using the palm of my hand and with the other, grab him by the hair. I wheeled over to a pillar and slammed his head against it.

Let's tango.

"Agh!" he winces with what looks like mango or peach in his nose. Cat then comes in and takes out her hidden fruit cup and does the same, only this time she wraps her ankle around his leg to make him fall.

"I grew up as a fighter, too." She smiles and winks.

While the other boy tries to get up, boy number one then tries to run with a fisted hand that I dodged. Cat in return goes behind him and shoves the boy to where he loses his sense of balance and falls right against the same pillar. When his back faces us, I take the opportunity to grab the end of his shirt and pull it over his eyes. "I can't see! Derek, help me!" he yells, as his hands are flailing in the air.

I grab both of his wrists and bend them to his sides, forcing him to kneel before me.

Sounds of "oohs" and "ahhs" played in the background. People now began to stare.

With vengeance in mind, the boy's friend who claims to be Derek swoops in angrily and tries to grab Angela's hair as she and the girl with the hijab are just about to make it to the elevator.

"Angela!" Cat yells as she tries to warn Angela. She seemed to get the message because just as Angela turned around, she punched him right in the face. "This is why I don't like fighting," Angela says as she winces. The punch knocked the boy out and left a red mark on her fist.

"Nice, a black eye." Cat smiles in approval, examining the boy.

Both Cat and I cheered as we all began to make our way back to the table. While Cat and I gave people high fives, Angela continued to comfort the girl with the beautiful floral hijab and chestnut eyes. Her hands stopped shaking, and she looked happier.

I have to admit, Angela's touch of friendliness was beyond my skill set.

When we got to the table, I heard Kim mutter to Xander "Looks like we got a new member after all," as he gazed at his food before taking another bite.

"Welcome to the group, guys, this is…"Angela pauses for a second and looks at the girl.

"Bea," the girl says.

Everyone waves and makes room for her to take a seat. "You don't have to move. I have a few friends who are probably looking for me. So, I'll be on my way." Bea tells us.

"Well, you're welcome to join us anytime," Xander says as he takes a bite of his food. A small blush surfaces on Bea's cheeks. She smiled at us and waved as she was leaving.

"So, about the plan-"

The speakers briefly turn off and turn on with the voice of the same person as before. "Breakfast is over. Please stand still for your companions."

Kids began to run around and scream, but we all knew it was futile every time.

9

In the first half of the day, I caught the eyes of my comrades. I spotted Cat in my math class and Angela and Kim in the hallways. Xander noticed me in the elevators, and as usual, his companion would roughly manhandle him. I still found it strange how he was one of the rare people to be handled so aggressively.

What could he have possibly done to end up like that?

At first, I was scared, but the more I got to know him, the easier it was for me to develop some sympathy. I would always try to mouth "It's gonna be okay" whenever I felt like it was the right time. He'd send a silent thank you and carry on with his malicious companion.

At the start of every class, it would be the same as the previous. The teachers would scan us with holograms, re-introduce themselves, explain, and then proceed to teach new material. I was still surprised by my placement. It felt intimidating. Some students would glower at our smartness while the teachers preach to us. At least I didn't feel alone knowing others had similar placements. By the end of class, my brain would often feel like mush. There was still much to learn, yet little to no brainpower was left for me to use. I was only a worksheet away from getting another migraine. At the times when I couldn't think anymore, I would lean back and look around.

As I analyzed my surroundings, I noticed the absence of windows. There would be clocks now and then telling the time, but the date and destination were still a mystery. It could've been a Tuesday or a Saturday. We could be in the middle of Livery Island, for all I know. There weren't any calendars in the classroom, either. It could be someone's birthday and they probably wouldn't know it unless an announcement was made. Looking back from the day Max and I were taken, I could only assume that about a week or so had passed.

By the time lunch came by, I was starving, mentally drained, and deeply needed to use the restroom. "Where's the restroom?" I asked Charles while doing the potty dance.

Yes, the potty dance. I needed to go that badly.

"We're almost at the cafeteria." He responds, not giving me a second glance.

"I am going to pee my pants," I say bluntly back.

He raises an eyebrow and glances at his GPS device. Instead of going to the elevator, we make a turn into a hallway and stand in front of the restroom doors with four other guards waiting outside. "Be quick." He snaps.

I nod and enter.

The restroom was surprisingly clean and tidy. Near the last stall was a cupboard filled with feminine hygiene products and small snacks. A girl was reaching inside it before entering the stall. In the process of doing my business, I listened to two different girls talk to each other.

"You saw it too, right?" A girl says out loud in her stall.

"The TV broadcast?" questions girl number two.

"Yeah."

"I heard someone tried to escape." A third girl randomly says.

There was a silent pause between them. A girl sighs before leaving the stall.

They spoke among themselves, whispering the details, but the most I heard was that the person failed and was most likely not seen again. Apparently, the person who attempted to escape wasn't the only one who disappeared, many of the other children did as well.

"I want to go home." One of them murmurs while washing her hands.

Me too.

I can't imagine living here until I reach eighteen. It sounds like an absolute nightmare. No more movie nights. No more road trips. No more family time. That would all be replaced by what they wanted us to do.

By the time I got out of the stall to wash my hands, one of them began to sob. It was an emotional moment that reminded me that I needed to be fuerte to survive. I leave the restroom, thinking back to the broadcast. I knew things were tense, but I hadn't realized how terrible it was.

In fact, mom and dad never liked us looking at the news.

"The media doesn't always tell the entire story." My mother would tell us. She would list various examples and slowly progress into a tangent of the wrongs in the world. My father would agree and explain the gravity of the situation. He would be concise about the important details and at the same time contrast what was said versus what he believes is happening. The first time they sat down with us and turned on the news was when they started taking away kids from the schools. They wanted us to see what was going on and explain why we couldn't go to school anymore. First, they came after the foster children, then the ones with single parents, and finally, every single kid.

We were so careful, but in the end, they still found us.

"Go," Charles tells me when we reach the cafeteria doors.

I grab a plate of food and head up to the same spot where Angela and the group meet.

Surprisingly enough, Kim and Xander were the first to be at the table. They were discussing something in hushed voices and stopped mid-conversation when they noticed me.

"Anything you guys want to spill?" I say with a smirk.

They both stared at me, bewildered by my sudden personality. I was hardly an expressive person, but when I am, it gets interesting. "Spill? What spill? We didn't spill anything?" Xander replies, playing dumb. He'd be a terrible actor if he were one.

"Uh-huh. Sure." I say bluntly. "It's fine. I shouldn't be a chismosa."

Kim glances away from his food and asks, "A samosa?"

"Cheese- moh-sa. It's slang for someone who is nosy." I explain. Both of them were amused and together we broke out in laughter. When we calmed down, that is when Xander tried to clear things up. He elaborates that they were talking about something super private but can't explain it in full detail until they think it is the right time. I can see it in their eyes that they are holding back, yet feel hesitant in doing so. It was almost as if they were unsure if they were able to trust me. Honestly, I don't blame them. We just met yesterday, and I still feel standoffish. I can see where they're coming from.

"Hello, beautiful people!" Angela and Cat cheer. They both sit down with their plates of food.

I take a bite from my plate, as hungry as I could be. This time, I chose a classic pepperoni pizza, a small salad, and a stack of french fries. Surprisingly, it wasn't all as greasy as I thought it would be.

Suddenly, as we resumed our conversation, Angela speaks in a very low voice.

"Okay everyone, real talk." Angela's eyes darkened and her smile lines diminished. There was something about her demeanor that completely shifted from usual. "Did you see the broadcast?"

To any ordinary person, it was a simple question. In this scenario, the simple question implores something deeper. It was written all over their faces.

Kim flickers his gaze to me and back to Angela. His shoulders tensed, and it felt as though there was a silent conversation between them. Somehow, this became a battle, and I was watching from the front line. Xander plays with his chains, shifting them loudly. I take a few fries and put them in my mouth.

Everyone is staring at me except for Kim. I gave a small nod, unsure of what to say to her. The music blaring in the speakers felt a little louder.

"I did too." Cat signs. She gnaws on a slice of watermelon, completely unbothered. Kim and Xander both look away and give small, slight nods. We all take another bite of our food, and Xander drinks water out of a small disposable cup.

"I think we all did," Kim states. He angrily looks at a piece of broccoli that stands on the end of his fork.

"Okay, so who thinks Ella should join us and the rest of the Allies?" Angela says suddenly.

At the mention of the Allies, water spouts out of Xander's mouth like a kettle. He coughs a little before giving Angela a not-so-jolly glance. Kim and Cat exchange expressions as if they were having an internal conversation. If I were to put their dialogue into words, it would follow the lines of Kim scolding Cat, while she nonchalantly supported Angela's decision. Their little plan is why they were late to meet us at the lunch tables.

"I'm serious. Our days are being numbered and there is only so much we can do with the group we have now. You all saw what was happening in the broadcast. There's strength in numbers. I know you guys were thinking the same thing this morning." She reasons.

"Besides, you're always asking for new recruits, Xander. How am I supposed to do that with so little time and so many people? You guys always are so picky of who we can or can't trust." She says, this time facing Xander. He seems almost conflicted by the facts Angela was stating.

"But we can't expose everything! Who knows if we can trust her? Angela, you know there's a reason why we're *selective*." Kim mutters, loud enough for everyone to hear.

He was direct. I give him that. He never seemed to cut corners and kept to himself unless Cat was by his side. She was always his soft spot. They would often whisper in hushed voices and stay seated next to each other whenever they could. If someone was on Cat's right, he would be on her left, and vice versa. As for the rest of the table, these guys were very tight-knit, which is why I felt like such an intruder.

Back home, I would always avoid these types of groups. I hated the way they had their eyes on me and the disgust they displayed when I didn't meet their social circle expectations. I liked it better when I bounced around and randomly befriended like-minded individuals on the spur of the moment.

"Maybe I should just-." I slowly get out of my seat, keeping myself at ease.

I don't deserve to sit here and be judged, especially by someone equally skeptical.

It was just like the time everyone accused me of liking Nick when he was with Stephanie. All eyes were on me. Funny enough, Nick was the one who spread the rumor on the playground and clearly had a crush on me.

Let's just say that was a sticky situation that ended with a heartbroken Stephanie, detention, a meeting with the principal, and a black eye. Not to brag, but the one I gave Nick was worse than mine.

Angela gets a firm grasp of my elbow, stopping me from moving. "Wait." She mouths to me.

"Please don't involve me." I mouth back and shake my head.

"Okay let's vote." She says as she raises her hand proudly in the air. This seemed to make Kim upset, but he still stayed seated. "Any other votes?"

Hesitantly, Xander and Cat raise their hands, while Kim takes a bite of his broccoli. Cat gives him a nudge, but it seems like he is firm with his decision.

"Alright, it's three against one. Majority rules." Angela announces.

Kim, however, frowns and picks at another object on his plate. Cat seemed to be very upset with him. She got up with her food and switched seats with Angela. Not gonna lie, I felt a little disappointed that Kim did not raise his hand, but I can also understand from his point of view.

"Perfect. Now what is it that you would like to know since I'm assuming you're still a newbie?" Her eyes drift off to my arm. Edges of the bandages poked on the side of my short sleeve. They didn't bother me as much as they used to. I found comfort in the bandages, as it felt like a small hug.

I purse my lips, practically tongue-tied. Not because I didn't have questions, but more so because I didn't know where to start.

"I'll go over the basics." Xander intervenes.

He starts by explaining our outfit color and the way we are handled. "We are colored coordinated by our age. I think Cat figured out most, if not all, the age ranges."

I look at Cat and give her a thumbs up. She smiles at me and resumes giving Kim the cold shoulder.

The blues range from ages eleven to fourteen. The older the person is, the darker their uniform becomes. This explains why Xander wears a dark blue outfit, and we wear baby blue. Anything from fifteen to eighteen wore pink, and those who were younger than eleven wore purple and green.

Here's the part that had me shaken in my seat.

They both glanced at my arm and questioned me. "Did you arrive here conscious or unconscious?"

At first, I found that question to be strange until I remembered how I got here. I've gotten so used to seeing kids with bandages that it just became something oddly normal.

They looked at each other and simultaneously said, "Unconscious."

"When you arrive here, they put this thing on your head, it measures your range of intelligence. That's how we got assigned to our classes. Of course, you wouldn't know if you arrived here unconscious. What they said in the classroom about allocating you based on test scores was a lie," Xander says.

So, you're telling me, they put a thing on my head, put on these clothes, given medical care with who knows what medication, while I was asleep! I could only imagine Max's reaction to all of this when he came here, that is, if he woke up after fainting. I pray that he had a better arrival than I did. He's been through enough nightmares.

"What exactly is this thing your guys are planning that you want me in?" I ask, raising my eyebrow.

"Before we get to the Allies, do you have any other questions?" Angela speaks this time.

I felt like I was pretty much filled in. The tracker on my foot seemed to be self-explanatory, along with the classroom assignment and the use of holograms. There's not much to ask about the companions other than their personal information. A small part of me still wanted to ask about Xander and his situation with the chains, but that would be too invasive on my part. I should also probably talk to Kim at some point if he does have any suspicions about me. Judging by Cat's nonchalant reaction to all of this, it seems like she knows a whole lot more than what she is letting on. Everyone was holding in something, and they knew I knew.

The speakers above them ring sounds of the same female voice announcing everyone to wait for their companions to collect them, stopping the conversation.

Newcomers like me on the floor below us began to panic and run, banging on the doors of the exit. One girl with brown hair and glasses searches the crowd, yelling a name and shoving against the force of the crowd. Grabbed by the hand, she is dragged out the same way I had been when I found Max in another cafeteria with children his age. Soon enough, they too will learn the hang of things as I did. Here you have to, to survive, to stay sane.

Like yesterday, begrudgingly, Charles takes me to Ms. Charlotte's class and instructs me to behave with a threatening gaze. I returned the gesture and turn away.

Thankfully, in today's class session, no one was hit since Ms. Charlotte did most of the talking by explaining the fundamentals of sentence structure and diction. After the lesson, the class was filled with the sounds of pencils tapping and murmurs while we worked on the worksheets she gave us. She then proceeded to provide a study guide for the companions to give us at the end of the day.

"I suggest you memorize it if you want to stay in this class." she precautions, her face numb underneath the heavy makeup she wore.

Watching the study guide handed over to their companions, most of my classmates tense, strengthening their spines and taking shaky breaths. Next to me, I see a boy completing his worksheet and stuffing it underneath his salmon jumpsuit. Following him, the girl in blue two rows ahead cleverly stuffs the folded paper into her hair and latches it into place with a bobby pin.

Feeling anxious about their behavior, I peek at Xander who has already concealed his worksheet. His eyes answered telling me, "Hurry," and gestured for me to tuck it in my jumpsuit.

Did I miss something? Why is everyone so tense? What's in these papers that are so important to keep them?

As though my life depended on it, I quickly folded the worksheet into a small square and kept it in place with my bra strap.

"Good luck, children," Ms. Charlotte murmurs to herself in an empty classroom, smiling ominously.

Heading to the gym, or in this case, passing the gymnasium, we all noticed ropes were hanging from the ceiling. It seemed like we were supposed to climb them, but the G.C.P.O.A. had other plans. Blocking the entrance of the gym was yellow tape and a line of officers wearing complete black. Upon arrival, they instructed our companions to relocate us outside to the basketball courts.

"Don't look," Charles warns far too late. Peeking in between the soldiers and into the gym, I saw a girl much older than me, along with a boy sharing very similar features as her hanging at the top with the rope wrapping around their necks. In the pocket of their clothes were study guides.

I take a short breath and send quiet prayers to the bodies I have just witnessed. There was no chance they were alive by the coloration of their bodies and the way they stayed there emotionless. Following my reaction, gasps and murmurs flood the halls as we are being taken outside.

We had to run various staircases to get to the back of the building, which led us to the outside. Coach Mike put us into teams and ushered our companions back inside, annoyed. Thankfully, Cat and Angela were on my team along with the blond girl with acrylic nails that hit me with the dodgeball yesterday. Right as she recognized me, she apologized and briefly introduced herself. Her name is Rebbeca. The last member of the team was the boy who lost his tooth, Cameron. The five of us went against other teams in the giant courtyard.

Taking a breath of fresh air relaxed my lungs, as it was thankful to be outside, but my mind had its own storm. Past the barbed wires and fences were miles and miles of the forest surrounding the facility. There was a watch tower covering every corner, most likely filled with a handful of officers. A few of them were standing there overlooking us. They pointed their guns whenever we went close to the wires.

In front of the basketball courts stood the enormous skyscrapers, one of which I was living in. At certain points, the buildings are interconnected with each other, which explains all the twists and turns of the hallways. Coming in and out of the facility, past the wires, are trucks, buses with more children in them, and military vehicles. If there wasn't so much surveillance and challenges ahead, I would be more than happy to grab Max and get us home in one of those vehicles.

In between the games, Cat and Angela informed me to notify my companions to take me to the library during the free break time during dinner. If I wanted to be a part of the escape, I needed to meet them and the rest of the Allies there. The problem in my case is that the break time is when I eat with Max and his friend Mika. If I were to go missing without telling him, Max would be infuriated with me.

The library itself is perfect for meeting with the others since it is usually empty aside from the Allies members and studying students. It is also the place where they can obtain information about the facility among the books and access hologram pads to hack and surf the internet. Cat proudly tells me that she is the hacker of the group.

In the final rotation of the basketball games, we played against Xander and Kim's team. Walking over, I inform them that I'll go to the library tomorrow.

"Why tomorrow?" Cat signs. Meanwhile, Angela, Rebbeca, and Cameron play in the upper court fighting for the basketball.

"I don't want to worry my brother Max, I'll tell him I'll be gone next dinner so that he doesn't worry," I tell her jumping back on my feet as Kim runs to our side of the court, basketball in hand.

Cat nods her head, understanding my situation, and shoves Kim to get the ball away from his grasp. Coming from Kim's other side, I take the ball and run with it, bouncing it against the floor.

Xander spots me and blocks right in front of me. From the corner of my eye, I see Cameron waving his hands to catch my attention. I toss the ball over to him, and he catches it. The side of his mouth tilts upward as he takes a leap over Kim and shoots them into the basket.

In the background is a shrill of coach Mike's whistle. It was the end of the game and we won.

Pulling me aside, Xander tells me about the worksheets. "Study both the worksheet and the study guide today and tomorrow. Ms. Charlotte sets up one of them as a decoy so that the students in our class get taken. I would know since I've taken her exams." Xander explains.

"If your writing is not up to date and you don't carefully follow one of the prompts, you will be *relocated*." He warns.

"Relocated? What do you mean, relocated?" I ask, pressing for more details.

Xander swiftly peers at a watch tower and whispers, "They take you out. Kids who fail their classes will be 'relocated'."

Eyes widening, I search Xander's face for any type of expression. It was mostly hardened and furrowed as usual, but his eyes spoke plenty. They moved in certain distinct patterns that I admittedly enjoyed reading.

"You'll be fine."

"How do you know?"

"I just do," he replies.

But? There's a but somewhere in there.

Caught in between his words, his eyes slowly swayed to the lower half of his lashes and darkened with apprehension. "But it's Angela, I'm most worried about."

From what I've noticed, Angela often expressed to me that studies were not always her strong suit despite her ability to want to be a nurse like her mother. She never seemed strong in her academic capabilities, as she often hid behind her words of affirmation and charitable acts to reassure others she was doing fine.

She was not.

Xander told me she was a few points away during their last session from being shot on the spot. She was terrified.

When he pointed that out, I couldn't help but acknowledge how tightly she held on to her study guides and the way she peeked at them far too often with anchored eyes.

Much like Xander, I too was worried for Angela. I couldn't imagine being in the facility without seeing her face across the halls and up at the lunch tables.

"Be prepared for exams. You only have today and tomorrow. All classes hold these tests. That's why they give you two days." he cautions, glancing over his shoulder to keep an eye out for his companion.

Taking a deep breath, I walk over to Charles and head to my next class.

Another study guide was given.

By the time I got to Max, there by his side was Mika, with a plate full of pasta. The two sat down laughing while I got myself dinner. When I got back to the table, the two moved on to another joke they laughed about. Mika was wearing her headphones. She took them off so that she could hear both Max and I. I was surprised at how quickly she had gotten comfortable with me by the way she was able to muster out words or phrases and contribute to our conversation. It made me glad they felt safe, but also guilty about telling them.

"Erhm," I pause, waiting for the right moment to get their attention.

"I won't be able to join you guys for dinner tomorrow. I will be at the library since I have an exam in the next few days." I state as both of them watch me attentively.

"You got the study guide?" Max frowns, his voice cracking a little.

I nod.

"Only big kids get those. One of my classmates who had a big brother got the study guide. He failed and got taken away." Max murmurs in a low voice, squeezing the baseball in his hand. "He says he never saw him again after that."

Noticing his expression, Mika gets concerned.

"That's why I'll study hard at the library, so that doesn't happen," I said, touching his shoulder and reassuring Mika.

"Promise?"

"I promise."

"No, I don't want just any promise." He frowns.

"Again? Max, we can't always be making these promises, otherwise, it loses its significance."

"Please." He pouts his lip.

"Fine." I sigh, lifting my finger next to him. It was our seal to the unbreakable promises. We so far had a good streak.

"I pinkie promise," I say, curling my pinkie over his. "That I-"

"Pinkie, promise you'll be fine."

"I pinkie promise *we'll* be fine," I emphasize the 'we' part with a recurring smile, tugging his finger tightly against mine. We lower our hands and release, snapping our fingers.

When it was time to leave, Mika walked up to me with a small strawberry tart cupped in the palms of her hands. She hands me a piece before returning to her officer. Max waves to her and we head back to our rooms.

"Go wash up and brush your teeth, Max."

He frowns at my request and does as he is instructed.

Cautiously, I turned on the TV for any broadcasts that may indicate the outside world. I was met with disappointment as I was surfing through the channels and nothing important was displayed. At one point, there was slight static, but that was about it. The channel flickered to its original station and maintained its hold on the screen. I despairingly slouched on the couch and pressed onto the next.

"Anything new?"

"No," I answer plainly.

"Hey! Why do you have those, and I have basic blues?" I comment, jealous of his variety.

"I don't know. I have these and the other ones like yours." Changed into his purple truck-patterned pajamas, he walks out with his baseball planted in his left hand. He sits next to me on the couch and suggests we watch an episode of "Outwardly Stars" where Steven the Dog helps to save his friends from the evil squirrel, Dominic. He kidnapped each one of his dog friends and hid them in his secret lair.

He didn't last long as Max fell asleep beside me halfway through the episode. Without making a ruckus, I head to his room and grab a blanket to drape over him. I sat there keeping him company while I used the lighting of the TV to analyze the various study guides hidden in my jumpsuit.

I started with Ms. Charlotte's class.

12

"Ack!" I moaned as I rolled over to my side and fell on the floor. The side of my hip got the worst out of the impact. As for my back, a few of the study guides scattered on the floor cushioned my fall. As Max got ready, I hurriedly tried to grasp every detail and information I could review within the pages on the ground.

"How the hell am I supposed to remember all of this?" I wine.

"Are you allowed to take notes?" He holds up a pen he found in his room and a notepad.

"Well, they never said I couldn't. Otherwise, that would be-" The light bulb goes on. "Max, you're a genius!"

I take the pen and come to the alternative of writing the questions and answers on my arm, including the ones I have yet to solve. Noticing the writing on my wrist as she examined my arm, Esmeralda forced me to scrub it off. She hovered over me as each letter, equation, and passage flooded the sink with black ink. Max scowled at Esmeralda as they made their way out the door.

"That's not fair!" He exclaims.

She guides him to his companion. "You're sister is smart. She doesn't need to write on herself. It's not allowed."

Max stomps his feet and together we carry on with our day. It was the same old, except for when all the sympathetic teachers reviewed their questions in the study guide. You can effortlessly tell which of them cares for their students and which of them doesn't. The ones who didn't care watched us struggle to sneak away any worksheets that had to be returned. In those classes, my eyes couldn't tear away from the contents on the whiteboard, for I was afraid the information would disappear within seconds. A small indentation on my thumb formed from all the times I dug the pencil into my skin.

When it got to lunch, none of us could stomach our food and spent the time studying among each other, scavenging for answers to our questions. We all tried to make the most out of our limited free time and hid the papers in our clothes when it was time to leave.

In gym class, papers scattered on the floor, slipping out of pockets and sleeves. We attempted to quickly sweep them up before the coach got to them first.

To get them back, he required the poor students to beg on their knees, otherwise, he would rip it to shreds or keep it to himself like some achievement. To the girls, like an utter creep, he would ogle at us while we crouched. He somehow got away with positioning himself behind the unfortunate ones who weren't fast enough.

He almost did that to me.

I was too horrified and left a single piece of paper on the floor rather than allowing him to come close. Thankfully, that was the only paper I lost as I had all the other ones held together inside my jumpsuit through a series of paper clips and pins, I stole from the classrooms and teacher desks. When you're as invisible and quiet as me, no one tends to notice you. It's how I got away with so much as a kid.

Xander saw my technique in one of our classes and nodded in approval. Angela was smart to fold hers into small origami figures and tuck them into her clothes and shoes. She, too, secured them with paperclips. Cat, on the other hand, was a genius. She stayed up last night sewing pockets onto all of her jumpsuits. It was one of the many reasons why she slept during lunch. She made sure to always have something on her. At one point, I saw the tip of a pocket knife poking out of her left pocket during chemistry class. When she noticed my gaze, she sunk it deeper into her pockets and placed a finger to her upper lip, gesturing to me to keep quiet.

I gave her a nod and continued to focus back on the lesson on the board. When it got to dinnertime, I instructed Charles to take me to the library. He raises a single eyebrow with great suspicion.

"Stay out of trouble." He reprimands authoritatively.

Much to my surprise, he drops me off and waits outside while I enter the library. I couldn't help being in awe, as it was bigger than the public library I often went to. At the end of every aisle was a cart filled with holotablets, something I dreamed of using. They were much too expensive where I was from. Papers and pencils were all that I had to get me through my education. The others in my pretentious classes taunted me with their high-tech tablets and computers.

It didn't bother me. My parents could afford what they could, and it did the same job, only less cool.

As I weaved my way to the back of the library, I found the fantasy section. My favorite section. On the floor next to a pile of books was Xander sitting criss-cross applesauce on the floor, smiling at a page he was reading.

At first, he didn't notice me approaching him until I sat down next to him.

"What are you reading?"

"Poetry."

"Poetry?"

"Yes, laugh if you'd like." He puts the book down and gathers the pile of books next to him. On his feet were heavy chains attached to each other leading to his hips, affecting his mobility.

"I wasn't going to laugh. I was just…."

"Surprised?" His chains jingle.

"Yeah. I don't know many people who like poetry, or um, read it."

"Do you?"

"Do I what?"

"Do you like poetry?"

"Depends on who the poet is," I shrug.

"I see." His gaze lowered to the book he was reading. He gently puts it back on the shelf and piles the rest he carried at his waist.

"Is it just you here? Where is everyone else?"

"They are uh, in a reserved room at the back of the library. I'll take you there. They should be starting the meeting soon."

"Okay," I reply, swaying my arms at my sides. "So, the Allies? That's what we're called?"

"Yes. I didn't pick the name."

"Who did?"

"Cat. She likes simple code words and finds it better than saying the Homing Herd." He snorts as we start to slowly walk out of the section. With each step he took, the chimes of the chains would echo against the shushed bookshelves. It was very awkward as I didn't have a clue as to what to say to him. He seemed almost bothered by my presence as if he didn't want me there. I could tell by the way he was pacing, but that only slowed us down.

"I know you don't trust me." He said suddenly.

"Huh?"

"I see the way you move away and look at me sometimes." He pauses and waits for me to say something.

I don't.

Every response I could think of sounded terrible like "Yeah I thought you were scary" or "My bad". I was always terrible with confrontation, especially when I couldn't hide behind lies. My truths were often far too harsh for the occasion. You can say I wasn't exactly the most consoling or sociable person. That's what was the main difference between Max and me.

He followed his heart, and I followed my head.

"I wasn't going to vote for you, but because Angela, I did… She was the first person who saw me as a human being. I trust her judgment more than anything." He continues.

"I see," I say, gazing at his chains. "In all honesty, I try not to judge, but the chains make it a tad bit difficult. I mean, I'm not afraid of you *anymore* and you don't have to explain yourself, either."

"Anymore?"

"I was at the start. Angela said you might bite."

"She did?" he chuckled.

"Yes, but after a while, you weren't so scary."

"I can quickly change that."

"How so?" I tip my head to the side.

He takes a heavy breath and hoists the books in his hands higher to his face.

"The reason I'm in these chains is because I killed an officer."

"What was the reason?"

"What?"

"I said, what was the reason?" I shift my eyes in his direction.

He blinked, eyeing me, completely dumbfounded.

Sure, I was a judgmental person, I won't deny that, but it was evident there was more on his end. I wanted to know his full story. He hasn't given me a reason not to.

"Go on, tell me," I say. "I won't judge. We are the victims, Xander."

He lowers his eyes, and I take a book from his pile.

"When they started to invade homes," he pauses, "my father had taken my two younger brothers with him to cross the border back to our country. I, on the other hand, needed to stay with my mother to watch over her and my infant sister."

"Okay."

"Essentially, I was the man of the house. We'd figured we wouldn't be taken away because she's a baby and I would leave when they reach the border." He sighed.

"And then what happened?" I opened up the book I took from him.

Xander closes his eyes and firms his grip on the books he holds.

He told me about how he hid in his home, similar to how Max and I did. He slept in the back of the shed of an apartment they were living in. He waited for further notice from his father and brothers, but they never called. He knew something was deeply wrong and assumed they were caught at the border.

"We came to this country when I was ten, believing we were safe from war. We didn't know it would go this bad. I waited a few more days for them to tell us they had arrived. We were going to go after them, but then…"

"Then the G.C.P.O.A. arrived." I finished the sentence for him. He nods his head and takes a shaky breath.

"On the day I was taken, I was in the shed taking a nap when I heard my mother scream. I got up and saw my little sister being ripped out of her arms. I-I I panicked and grabbed a shotgun from the shed. Next thing I know, I'm aiming it at them, and the trigger goes off."

He tells me the most graphic details of his first kill and the sound that came out of his apartment walls. When the soldier dropped his sister after being shot, she died onsite. His mother was too late to catch her.

Right there and then he was tackled on the ground and beaten to the point where he lost consciousness.

"That's why I'm in these chains. I'm a killer. A murderer."

"Xander, you did what you could-"

"I shot them."

His eyes began to tear up. It's almost as if he had been waiting for someone to tell him this. Waiting for reassurance of some kind. The books in his shaken hands slipped from his grasp and fell to the ground.

"You didn't mean to cause her death. You just wanted the soldier to leave your family alone. They're the reason why we're in this mess!"

"I know," he murmurs. "But we can't deny I didn't take away two lives, Ella."

"None of this would've happened if it wasn't for them. You are a victim. We are victims."

"Then why do I feel like this? Why am I like this!" He holds his arms, jangling his chains in front of my face.

"Because they have failed to protect us!" I shout to him.

My words carry through the library and bounce against its silent walls. We stood there frozen in place until we heard another member enter the library. Coming to my senses, I crouch down to the floor. He does the same.

"What do you plan to do when we escape?" I question, quietly collecting the books at my feet.

He turns a corner and picks up some of the books I missed. "I want to find out what happened to my family."

I nod my head, and we make our way to a door at the back of the library. Xander taps the door cryptically as if he were sending a signal. The door opens, and he stops me.

"One last thing." He whispers. "Don't let Kim get to you. Just like me, he too has his reasons why he didn't vote to keep you in."

"I know. That is why I am here to prove why I should be in there." I duck under his arm and enter the spacious room.

13

Too many eyes were on us. They all froze into place and resumed once they felt assured enough by Angela who closed the door behind us.

In the center of the room was a round table filled to the brim with books and projections that came out of holotablets. Navigating the material Xander had given them are Cat and Kim hovering over the table.

Angela sat in her chair and gestured to me to go sit on the floor as all the chairs in the room were taken over. I take my place beside her and focus my attention back on the table.

"Alright everyone," Kim says, silencing the room of all chatter.

"According to Cat's latest intel with the outside, we have little to no time to waste. The plan is to escape a week from now." He announces projecting what is supposed to be a map of the facility and its surroundings. Cat remains silent tapping the holotablet vigorously.

It was quite obvious she was the brains behind the mission. I can only imagine how exhausting and terrifying it must be to handle her level of information while we are under constant scrutiny.

In a couple of whispers, Angela had expressed to me how Cat is essentially our ticket out of here. It verified most of my assumptions of I had of her. After all, like most animals, the silent ones are always the most potent.

She is the one who stays up late at night maintaining contact with the outside and spends the rest of the day resting her eyes, especially during lunch. Her common tasks consisted of hacking the surveillance camera using the holotablet she was given and making sure what was said in the room, stays in the room.

On occasion, Cat too had other assignments she did not disclose until she finished them. Angela didn't know how Cat could do it, but at one point, Cat was able to slip out of the facility and return the next day completely unnoticed. Though, she did get a few bullet scars and bruises from her journey.

"Is there any way for it to be done tonight? Exams are tomorrow! Last time, we were provided answers!" complains a boy leaning against the wall.

Kim shakes his head running his fingers through his hair out of frustration. "After our last attempt, our contact has been limited, meaning there will be no test answers. We must fight to stay here until then, as we cannot afford to mess up any more of our escapes." He responds assertively while hovering over Cat's shoulders, eyeing the holotablet.

"Anything else?" Angela speaks over, inviting the others in the room to ask their remaining questions.

"I don't want to die!" another voice emerges from the room. A few more kids around me begin to panic, whipping out their study guides.

"I barely passed!" cried another voice.

Shouts rang around the room consisting of similar responses. Angela and Kim attempted to speak over them, but it had been too loud. Noticing their frustration, I moved away from my spot and grabbed a holotablet. With the holotablet, I climb onto a table and slam it to the ground, capturing everyone's attention.

They all stared at me with wide eyes of confusion. Cat included.

"Look, I'm scared too! This is my first time taking these tests. Right now, our best bet is to compare these study guides and utilize them. If we continue to argue, we'll be wasting time that we could've used to make sure we don't end up in a grave!" I exclaim, my face hot and red as a cherry.

"Oh yeah? What good do you know, new girl?" A boy emerges from the crowd.

"Enough to keep my brother and I alive. Unless YOU have a plan to get us out of here, I insist you stop your horrible attempt of provoking me and listen." I lower myself to the ground and pass through them sitting in my corner. Their eyes wandered on me.

"So, what's the escape plan?" I turn my head to Cat. Her fingers hovered over the tablet.

She smiles and gestures to Kim to continue back to the projected map. Without hesitation, he moves on and begins to explain. The crowd dies down and all return to their original positions in the room.

14

Hearing the knocks of our guards at the library door was more than enough to make me flinch. It took me back to the day that brought me here.

Funny how something so small had such power over me. It wasn't too long ago either. On our way back to our cells, Max and his guard crossed over to our path.

I couldn't help but stare at the bruise on Max's eye and the redness of his knuckles.

I have no idea what happened, but this was not okay, it was way out of his character if he did happen to get in a fight or cause any type of trouble. Every time he caught me staring, he would hide his hands, fix his hair to cover his eyes, and sway closer to his companion's side so that she was between us. It was bad enough that I was the only family Max had at the moment, I didn't want to make things worse with a scolding.

Yet, I was going to have to do it if I wanted to get any answers from him. He's too stubborn for his own good. I just hope he tells me without causing an argument or thinking that I was being nosy. The last thing I would want is for him to hate me.

When we finally get there, the doors close, and right on cue, Max tries to run to his room to avoid me.

"Max!" I yell as I follow him.

I knew him well enough to know that he was going to try to shut the door in my face. "Max! I am talking to you!" I say running a little faster to make it inside his room first. "You're not going to lock me out."

"You're such a cheater! You're always faster than me!"

"Because I'm your big sister. Tell me-"

"I don't want to talk about it!" He hisses as he tries to kick me out. I narrow my eyes in disapproval and sit down on the floor, maintaining my position.

He wasn't going to get rid of me so easily.

His face flushes to a maroon color and attacks me like a monkey. It didn't bother me too much considering that we used to rough house a lot or get into stupid arguments over who can have the last cookie or the TV remote. My parents were there to stop us from fighting. Without their guidance, I had to be the one to cool him down.

When he has just about enough from pulling, shoving, and tugging me, he grabs one of his baseballs and angrily lays flat on his bed with his face buried into the pillow.

"It's not fair, you fight people all the time! Your hand is red too! So why am I the one in trouble?" He muffles in his pillow.

"I don't fight people, I use self-defense, Maxine. And you're not in trouble, at least not yet." I correct him.

He makes a noise under his pillow that sounds like a growling werewolf.

"I'm going to take a shower. After I'm done, we'll talk about it and you better calm down. Deal?" I say it as if it were an option.

"Fine." He mumbles angrily in his pillow.

Just like I said, after I had taken a long shower and changed into a fresh new set of prison attire, I went back inside Max's room. Surprisingly enough he didn't lock me out. His doorknob glided freely at the palm of my hands.

"Spill," I tell him as I sit on the edge of his bed.

He opens his mouth as the pillow covers his face. "Mi-"

"Hold on, are you calm? I'm not going to have this conversation if you're not calm enough to tell me directly." I contend, addressing his bubbling ill-temper. "Do you need me to give you another minute?"

He sighs, inhaling and exhaling. "No. I'm calm."

"Can I see your face?"

"Ugh."

"If want, I can leave."

"No, no, I'll get up." He grumbles, holding the pillow on his chest with one hand and the baseball with the other. He seemed a bit reluctant as he made every attempt to avoid my authoritative gaze.

"Mika and I were in math class and there were these boys that kept making fun of her. They kept making fun of her because she's different." Max slowly says. He waits for me to react, but I let him continue.

"They kept calling her dumb because she doesn't talk and moves her hands in the air but that's what makes her comfortable. One of them pulled her pigtails so I punched him. After that, we got into a fight." He quietly says the last part clutching his baseball.

"And how did Mika react?"

He crinkles the middle section of his eyebrows almost as if he didn't expect me to ask the question.

"Well?"

"She didn't like it."

"That's understandable." I swiftly grab the stuffed Zebra that is on the floor.

"Are you mad, Elena? Are you gonna yell at me?"

I take the Zebra and set it down next to him, exchanging the zebra with a study guide I left on his desk.

"I'm not going to yell at you, Max."

"Why?"

"Because I would've done the same," I say, recalling back to my conversation with Xander.

Mouth agape, he pauses unsure what to say. He stares at the baseball in his hands and places it down, grabbing the Zebra instead.

"El, you're scaring me."

"Look, as long as we're here, you and I need to get along." I bend my knees to his eye level. "I'm going to need you to trust me these next few days," I state, unfolding one of my study guides. My eyes dart to the door and quickly back to him. It took some effort, but he eventually caught my drift. He kept his mouth closed and bobbed his head.

There was only so much I could freely say under the impression that the entire facility was bugged.

"I'll go ahead and leave you be. If you need me, I'll be studying in the kitchen."

"Wait!" he shouts, lifting himself out of his bed. He pulls out a small blueberry muffin wrapped in a paper towel. "You missed dinner. Mika and I saved it for you."

I thanked him and took it with me to the kitchen. It reminded me of the days when the roles were switched.

During the initial house raids, the government implemented a new system. Households may only purchase two meal servings, one for the father and one for the mother. It was a tactic to starve out families so that most would be willing to give up their hidden children.

The first week was rough. I remembered how often Mami and Papi would try to hide their growling stomachs from us, pretending they weren't hungry. I insisted we rotated each day so that none of us would starve. They agreed with my proposal, but on the days when their meals would come, they would each eat half of the platter and give the rest to Max and me. When I declined, they would scold me and insist I eat right in front of them.

Things turned for the worse when the rations became scarce. Like my parents, I pretended to not be hungry and gave my brother the remainder of my share for him to eat. That same day, I snuck out at night and made my way to our garbage bins. I saw both of my parents there eating what they could find and returning to their beds with something in a black bag. I grabbed a rotten fig from the tree and ran to my room.

When morning came, I woke up to a smell similar to bacon. I knew it couldn't possibly be bacon, because to afford such delicacy would require the expense of an arm and a leg. We didn't have that type of money.

I sit at the table as my mother happily places a plate with eggs and some sort of cooked meat on the side. The eggs were probably stolen from the neighbors. They had enough chickens and eggs to allow a few to go unnoticed.

Max joins me, smiling ear to ear oblivious to my suspicions. My father enters the kitchen with two felt jackets of a raccoon's fur for us to wear in the winter.

I chew back my realization and proceed to swallow the raccoon meat. We play pretend, enjoying our meal.

It was enough to keep us alive.

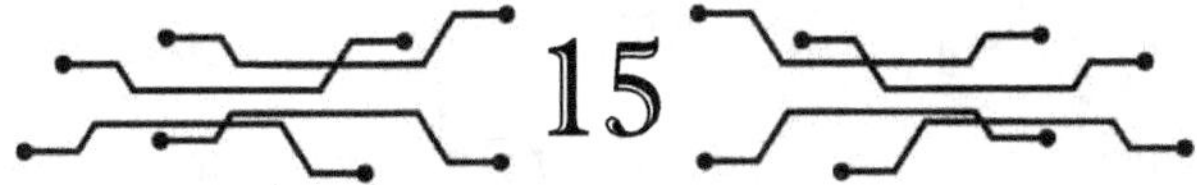

Max had to wake me up early.

He was afraid I'd oversleep and miss my chance to study the last few pages of the study guides I had left. I could only have it for so long until it was time for either Charles or Esmeralda to collect them.

"Study a little more. I don't want you to be taken away," he says, holding up one of my guides at the bridge of my nose. The poor kid was still in his pajamas with tired eyes and messy hair. It made me wonder if he slept at all last night.

"I won't be taken away, Maxine. We already pinkie swore remember?" I groan, pulling my bed sheets to the side. "But if it will get you to ease your nerves, I'll study."

He smiles at my compliance and plops the rest of the papers on my lap. I thanked him for his efforts, and as promised, I studied until it was time for Esmeralda to come and fetch me. She gave me ten minutes to surrender what I had. Luckily, I knew what to do. I managed to sneak a few miscellaneous papers inside the soles of my shoes and leave a few written notes I wrote inside the lining of my bra. In the bathroom, I tied my hair into a bun, tucking in small pieces of paper I ripped out from the study guide, and concealing each one with a pin inside my hair.

Esmeralda pats me from the chin and down until she is satisfied with me. She picked at my arm a few times and completely removed my old bandages.

"I will no longer be coming here. Your arm is as good as new. If you get hurt again, I will make your next recovery painful." she bitterly uttered to me, slapping my healed arm. I could tell she was nervous for me. Her body tensed at the crevices of her broad shoulders and her jaw lifted to a sharp point. It was her way of threatening me to stay out of trouble.

"I'll miss you too, Esmeralda." I wink. I follow her out the automated doors and walk with Charles to the cafeteria. He instructs me to hold his hand. I glare at him, keeping my hands at my sides stiffly. It was a subtle gesture of my rebellion.

"Just do it." He commands, standing beside me, refusing to press the elevator button. I roll my eyes and harshly place my hand over his balled-up fist. Unclenching and holding my hand normally, there was a faint sensation of a small material being slid in between them. It felt like tissue paper.

He presses the elevator button, and we enter. Inside the elevators were a few other companions holding their child's hands. Very little of them didn't. It wasn't anything new per se, but nonetheless, it was strange to me.

When we get off, Charles remains his usual stoic self, bidding no mind to the paper's contents in our hands. He evidently did not want to draw any attention to it. It had to be something bigger, something that is part of the resistance he is in. What else could it be?

I do my best to avoid the elephant in the room and keep our hands tightly clasped together, fearing the paper could somehow slip out. When we arrive at the cafeteria, I carefully scoop it out of the palm of his hands as I pull away from him. Holding my head up high, I walk into the cafeteria, tucking in the scrunched-up paper on the waistband of my pants. I peek, noticing its small inscriptions. In bold letters were my classes and underlined each one, were multiple choice answers.

At the tables, none of us uttered a word about the meeting. We all silently chew through the vitamins given to us along with our partnered breakfast meal. I don't bother mentioning the test scores.

The first exam was brutal.

Had I not been given the test answers, I would've surely failed. There was no denying it. None of the questions corresponded with the study guide the teacher gave us. In fact, he was beaten in front of us for giving us a study guide matching too much familiar content of the exam. Blood splattered everywhere as he struggled under the batons of the soldiers surrounding him. I bit the insides of my cheeks waiting for his screams to die out. When they did, they dragged out Mr. Posler's body, smearing the floor. A new teacher walked in grinning from corner to corner, slamming our newfound exams on each of our desks. All the questions were on our given holotablets.

When he approaches me, I force myself to stare at the desk to avoid any problematic interactions. One wrong look could make me his next target. I tremble in my seat, displaying my fear.

It pleased him.

"Your teacher was foolish for thinking you all have the potential to pass. Passing is a privilege." he gawked, smoothing the nonexistent hair on his head. He gleefully reclined in the teacher's chair, wiping off the blood from his brown shoes, displaying no signs of disgust. His cheeks lifted higher, pleased.

I sneakily submitted my given answers, recalling each letter I memorized off the tissue paper. When I was done, my holotablet gave a small buzz and submitted my answers, shutting itself off. A few more minutes passed, and the remainder of the holotablets did the same.

The teacher picks up his holotablet from his desk and starts to list off various names with a pitch of excitement. Those students are escorted from class, and the rest of those uncalled, remain seated in the classroom.

I was one of those seated.

Congratulations, you've earned the privilege to stay in my class," he announces, nodding in approval.

At least two-thirds of us remained untouched. I take a breath of relief, wrapping my hands around my waist, feeling the answers against my skin.

I relied on them for the rest of the day, that was until I landed in Ms. Charlotte's class. That was pure luck.

"I will decide who leaves and stays," she announces, causing an uproar in the classroom. My fellow classmates stood away from their seats slamming the desk down with their hands.

"That's not fair!" The boy next to me shouted.

Under pressure, Ms. Charlotte slams her ruler vigorously with one hand and picks up her holotablet with another.

I don't bother to react.

I sat there waiting for her judgment to land on mine. Rather than calling out names, she clicks on the holotablet and waits for a companion to come in. When they do, she instructs them to "get it over with".

I didn't know what was worse, having someone die in the same room as you, or letting your imagination have its works.

"I don't want to die!" Mason jumps from his seat, tipping over his desk to the ground.

Ms. Charlotte smiles tapping her holotablet. I heard the door crack open behind me, listening to its steps. I don't move. I don't turn my head to see what will happen to Mason. All I hear is him struggling until his body thuds to the ground.

He goes silent.

Ms. Charlotte nods in approval, continuing to press the tablet's screen. Following the taps are more officers pouring into the classroom. One officer walks right beside me, holding a needle in his hand. He holds down the boy in pink next to me and injects the clear fluid into him. The other officers repeat, and all of their bodies fall limp, one after another.

One could call it murder, but I call it genocide.

The thuds of their bodies might as well have been the rings of bullets. Both will scar me either way.

The boy next to me falls into a position where his face is turned to mine as I keep my head down. His eyes were drained of color, and his body was an empty shell without its soul. Lying open was his mouth of what could've been his last words. I shift my direction to the other side of the floor, providing some respect to the dead. I wished I knew his name so that he could've gone unforgotten.

I could've been him.

His guard was so close to me. I thought I was going to die. I should be grateful that I am alive, yet I wasn't. If anything, I was angry.

How could any adult bring themselves to decide on a child's life in such a way? Aren't they supposed to be the ones to protect us?

This shouldn't be real.

If I had the chance to put an electric collar on each of these individuals, I would. I'd press the controller various times so that they would understand the pain we endured. I'd do it for hours until they groveled down to my feet, begging me to free them.

If they had been in our shoes, none of this torture would have continued. These adults were sociopaths. Murderers.

They were no better than serial killers.

With little to no caution, they carry their bodies out, leaving the rest of us wearing shades of blue. She had purposefully failed all of those in pink. There was no doubt. They were wiped clean from the classroom.

Although I should be focusing on myself, I couldn't help but be worried for Xander. I found myself wanting to turn back to make sure he made it out alive.

I let the little optimism I had left carry my worries away and kept my head tilted down to the place Mason's body once laid. There was a small smudge of foam that escaped his lips. Its bubbles maintained their shape on the floor, acting as a replacement for blood stains. In a way, it was the last mark he made in the classroom aside from the frame of his glasses they neglected to pick up.

"Consider this as a warning for your stupidity." Ms. Charlotte comments, placing her ruler on her desk. "The next exam will test your capabilities. This one is simply for us to flesh out the *unfavorable* weak links."

Ms. Charlotte turns her attention to her holotablet with deep satisfaction. Her lipstick smudged her teeth, and her lashes fluttered.

Taking the chance, I use the tip of my foot to scoot the discarded glasses closer to me. Leaning onto the side of my hips, I reach for them as if I were to be tying my shoes and tuck them against the black security band on my ankle. I jumped in my seat at the sensation of an electric current coming out of the mechanism.

I force my lips shut from expressing any vocal reaction.

Hearing my desk and chair jumbling against the floor, Ms. Charlotte peers away from the holotablet, scanning for the person who made the noise. She turns her head in my direction with her tongue rolling to one side of her cheek. She pauses and slams her ruler on the desk furiously. This time we all jumped out of our seats, startled by her feral temper.

"Get out of my sight," she demands to the class, slouching in her cushioned seat.

I clench my fists at my side as I am escorted out to lunch. Usually, we'd have lunch before her class, but granted, nothing about this facility is predictable despite its stern structure.

Filling up the elevator and taking notes of those who survived, my heart sank. I wasn't surprised by the result, but that didn't mean it was right.

Much like the elevator ride, the hallways were as quiet as ever. If you listen, you can hear the footsteps of mice scattering the vents and rippling around the overlooked corners of the facility. It was eerie. All that was missing was a couple of killer clowns and-oh wait, we have Ms. Charlotte. Aside from her, I could imagine the number of ghosts of lost adolescent souls moping down the same pathway and filling up all the empty space.

Far too few of us were left, especially those in pink. I spotted a handful of them gathering together in the center of the lunchroom performing their ceremony to mourn those who had passed. They chanted loudly against the booming music pouring from the speakers.

We are the pinks.
Mighty and free.

We are the pinks.
Our blood stains like ink.

Our color should not matter,
And our people were shattered.

You have ruined our trust,
And this system is unjust.

We will shout and scream,
As we are human as we can be.

We are the pinks!

The Allies, I included, chanted with them from our tables. We held each other's arms and closed our eyes, showing respect to those who had died. Angela sobbed as she mourned for them. It reminded her that had they not been deliberately eliminating the pinks, she would've been gone. She was next, that she knew.

Cat attempted to reassure Angela by saying she would seek out a study guide with answers so that they may all survive. If she couldn't, Cat would take the risk of hacking into the system somehow so that Angela would not be chosen. Angela took her words to heart and gave Cat a weak smile.

Amid our chant, sirens blared, and our companions came rushing in. They held their guns at us, forcing every person to lay their bodies on the ground. All of them pointed their weapons at our heads.

Kim had to shove Cat down as she was unable to hear the commands among the sirens and screams inside the cafeteria.

Next to me, I felt Angela's body shake. Her eyes shut tightly as a vault, and her hands spread open as if she were reaching for someone. When she caught my hand, her body shook less.

We waited there for at least an hour till the sirens had gone off. All our companions put away their weapons and ushered us back to our rooms in a quickened fashion. The corner of Charles's left eye twitched and darted upon arrival at our door.

He shoves me inside without any explanation, and I wait there, anticipating Max's arrival.

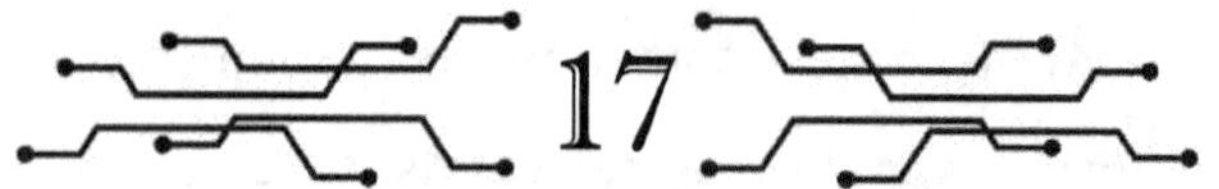

Borne on the back of his unamused companion, is an unconscious Max. She informs me to stay away from them, and I do… kind of. I keep my distance from them at his bedroom doorway as she tucks him in.

"What happened to him?" I asked her, using my body as a barrier.

I wasn't going to let her leave without giving me any explanation. I needed to know what happened to my brother. I couldn't tell if he was merely asleep or if he had been injured and was put into a coma. Either way, I was deeply concerned.

She wedges her arm over my clasped hand and tries to move. I tightened my hold and persisted in asking her the same question. She crosses her arms and instructs me to get out of her way. I shake my head and maintain my position.

She grows annoyed and forcefully shoves me to the ground. I seize her boot, twisting it with my hand. She bites the side of her mouth and tries to kick me with the other. It hurt, but not enough for me to budge. I got too cocky and recklessly bent her ankle until it was completely counterclockwise.

CRACK!

"AUGH!" She howls, falling over to her side.

No.

Way.

I didn't mean it. I wasn't planning on breaking her leg. I thought that if I had twisted it slightly, she would stop hurting me. Flexing my fingers, I examine my strong hands as a jittery sensation flared in the center of the swirls of my thumbprint.

What have I done?

My back hits the wall, keeping me upright during my daze. All I could think about was how I had messed up big time. Never had I once fought an adult, especially not to this extent, but I guess that's what happens when I let my emotions get the best of me. My goodness, I am going to be in so much trouble. I broke Maxine's companion's foot. What do I do? It's not like I can fix-

"Take this you son of a-"

"Enough!" Charles storms in grasping her wrist as she is about to strike me with her electric baton.

The shine of the electric light coming out of the baton was far too close to my throat, as I could feel the heat bursting out of her weapon. It buzzed like a hive full of venomous wasps, swarming to attack with their stingers.

"Charles?" She turns her head to him, eyes widened. "This little she-demon broke my ankle! She needs to be taken care of."

"Monica, this is a child we're talking about. My child. Only I may discipline her." He rips the baton from her clutches and tucks it inside his utility belt. "Go to break before I report this to HQ."

"But-"

"NOW!"

"Yes sir!" She staggers, sucking in air between the crevices of her teeth, taking her leave. She glares in my direction right when Charles shuts the door.

A smirk weaves its way on my face and quickly disappears when Charles commands me to sit down in the living room chairs.

"And you! Don't you think we're done here because we are far from that! How can you be so idiotic? I told you to lay low and to behave yourself! Do you have any idea how much trouble you have caused?"

"I just wanted to ask her what's wrong with-"

"I don't want to hear it." he snaps. "Gosh, now I have to punish you otherwise my rank is at risk!" He vigorously rubs his temple and paces around me in his heavy leather boots.

"Shave my head."

"What?" He removes his pinched fingers from the top bridge of his nose and blinks at me.

"Shave my head or break my finger," I say holding up my pinkie to him. "Either one can be my punishment."

He flickers his brown and grey moons, considering my suggestion. I rise out of my chair and move to the bathroom, searching the drawers for a pair of scissors or any hair shaver of some sort.

"Don't bother, they removed all sharp objects," he comments down the hall. He yanks a small walkie-talkie from one of the pockets on his vest and murmurs a few short phrases into it.

Tucking the device in its original place, he turns on his heels, shifting the chair I was sitting in. He turns on the water and scoots me closer to the kitchen sink. Grabbing a bucket he found in the bottom-level cabinets, he fills it to the brim with water.

"Sit," he instructs me.

I place myself on the seat and tilt my head back. He lifts the bucket and swiftly dumps the ice-cold water on me. Drops of the cold liquid traveled down my neck and trailing my back. I shivered a little and felt the hairs on my arms jump.

The metal doors open, and Esmeralda comes in with an object wrapped in a white cloth. She graciously pulls the cloth away, and in all its uttermost impressive state lies a fine sharpened silver electric razor. He snatches the razor, barely acknowledging Esmeralda, and turns it on. Without hesitation, he sternly pinches the upper part of my spinal cord with one hand, and with the other, he dives the device into my scalp. Clumps of my dark hair fell past my ears onto the ground dropping like flies. I concentrated on the sound of the razor as I felt the way it wove itself around my head. Focusing on all the hair I have lost would do me no good.

When Charles finishes, he snaps the razor off and exits the room in silence. Esmeralda gives me a sympathetic smile and neatly tidies up any rough patches that need extra attention. Luckily, Charles didn't nick me too severely. He wasn't the best barber, but he also wasn't the worst. I had an uncle who had to go to the ER because he impulsively wanted to shave his head while he was drunk. He said he wanted to know what it felt like. Thirty minutes later, my dad had to go to the hospital to check up on him.

While Esmeralda neatly collects my hair from the ground with a sweeper, she suggests I take a bath and change into new clothes.

"I'll do it after you're gone," I reply as I briskly snatched a few items from her cart that I believed would be of some use to me. I tuck them carefully in my pocket when she turns her body towards me.

"Is there anything I can do for you?"

"Yes!" I smile eagerly.

She regards me with great suspicion. "What is it?"

"Tell me what happened."

She takes the strands of hair she collected from the floor and dunks them into the trash bin of her cart. The remaining pieces of myself escaped into the air and landed on my lap.

"Perhaps shaving your head was not enough of a consequence."

I scoff and pick up a strand of hair on my lap, examining its texture.

"I'm worried. He's unresponsive, and I don't know what is wrong with him."

"He was gassed."

"Why?"

"I cannot disclose that. I've answered your question, run along, child."

"When will he be back to normal?"

"By tomorrow morning." She answers, sweeping the remainder of the hair quickly and providing me with a baby blue head scarf. I take the kind gesture and tuck the scarf in my pocket.

Like Charles, she too rapidly flees from the room and shuts the metal doors to their original position. When all is clear, I quickly sprint to the bathroom to inspect the damage. All the hair I grew over the years was no longer bonded to me. I felt exposed yet somehow, in the process, slightly free. My plan worked. No officer, bully, or person could hold me down by my hair ever again.

I refuse to allow someone to use my body against me.

Touching my ankle, I remove the broken tracker, analyzing it delicately. Somehow, the glasses must've disabled its magnetic field. At least that's what I believe, after all, I'm not a scientist. Though, I do think I know someone who can, Cat.

I placed the broken tracker on my ankle as a decoy and headed into the shower. Without the worries of maintaining my hair, it was one of the quickest I've taken. There was no struggle and no need for me to grapple with my hairbrush. The less time I spend on my head, the better. It was one last thing for me to worry about. It allowed me to move without hesitation and brought upon a newfound motivation. Most importantly, it was freeing in a world I felt trapped.

When Max woke, he showered me with details of yesterday. He recalled hearing sirens blaring in his classroom and the companions entering with gas masks. They all simultaneously pulled out mechanisms that looked like guns and covered the room with smoke. He told me he couldn't remember anything that happened in between or what may have caused all of this.

Part of me knew it would have to do with the Allies in some way.

"I'm glad you're okay, Max."

"What's going to happen to you?" He asks me.

"What do you mean?"

"Did you pass your exams?" His eyes circle my bare head. I could tell he wanted to reach for it.

"Yes," I reply, unbothered.

"Good."

"I'm not going anywhere," I assure him.

"Promise?"

"I promise," I say. "I promise to be right by your side." I curl my finger over his and snap them when I pull away. A tension seizes my arm, reminding me of a specific inquiry.

"Max, remember when you broke your arm, and we had to go to the hospital?"

He nods his head.

"Did your arm ever feel *different*?"

"I could throw better," he replies, running to his room. He returns with two baseballs in his hands. An old one and a new one. He hands me the old one and keeps the fresh baseball. He presses down on the ball with his palm and finger with little to no struggle. The ball's seams rip open, and its insides unravel.

"How did you- never mind." I shake my head. "Go get changed, your companion should be here soon to pick you up."

"But-"

"We'll talk more later," I interject, and fall back under the sheets. The AC blasted through the air vents, making it nearly unbearable to leave my pillow and blankets.

He lets out a groan and stubbornly plops himself on my bed. If we were back home, I'd shove him off.

But we're not.

At least for the next few weeks.

I let him lie there and the two of us stared at the ceiling in silence. I thought about mentioning the plan to him but decided against it. It was too much for me to dump on him. He was just a kid.

Yet so am I.

While he was unconscious, I took the liberty to slide the metal piece of the glasses through his leg, replicating the exact procedure I did to remove mine. Right when the metal piece had made contact with the interior of the tracker, sparks flew from his ankle, causing Max to shift in his sleep. The tracker wailed and shut down as I expected it to.

I was thankful I didn't accidentally electrocute him. I checked his pulse to make sure of it.

Perfect. If we escape, they won't be able to track us. We were one step closer to home.

For the case I would need to use the metal frame again, I pulled and hid it underneath a floorboard. When it was time for us to separate, I followed Charles on our usual route. I don't bother to mention the sheet of answers he had given me nor the condition of my hair. We keep a silent truce between us and act as if we were strangers.

As we walked, I noticed how several officers were stationed at every given hallway and entrance. They all tightly held out their weapons, with a finger on the trigger. They were eager to shoot, though there was no sign or indication of any possible dangers to require such measures. Perhaps the Homing Herd had made a breach of some sort? An attack? An escape?

It was a good indication. The facility was breaking. Among the breaks, there is always a chance to escape through the cracks. All that is left is a big enough push for the facility to fall. Yet, I mustn't underestimate the enemy, they were just as forceful in sealing our fates.

Rather than being taken to the cafeteria, I am ushered into my first class. Trailing at our heels are nurses with brown paper bags. They place the bags on our desks and stand right in front of us until we finish consuming the vitamin pill.

I take it and let it disintegrate on my tongue. The nurse scans my mouth with a probe and nods in approval when she is done. When she leaves, I spit the unswallowed residue onto my hand and rinse it with the bottle of water they provided. Based on the previous Allies meeting, I knew exactly what to do.

Had I taken the vitamin, I would be prone to sedation. The pill was to weaken us. According to Kim and Cat, the two had taken the pill to chemistry class during their breaks and ran some tests on its components. Most of what they found was aspects of what a sedative contains. It explained why I had always felt tired by the end of the day.

"If we are to flee, we must be in our best shape," Kim explained, displaying the lab results on a holotablet for us to conceptualize.

Yesterday, we were supposed to hold our next meeting to evaluate our next course of action. It all fell through when the pinks were killed, and a breach was made to the facility.

New assignments were given, and companions were placed in and outside of bathrooms. There was no location or room where there wasn't at least one companion or staff member in the room monitoring us.

It all seemed as if they were testing the waters. They planted cameras in surrounding areas and removed access to the outside gym area.

Coach Mike had a fit as he didn't know what to do with us. Both his gymnasium and his outside activities were suspended. We were given no choice but to be escorted into an empty classroom and learn about why physical health was important.

Very ironic.

During that time, the Allies and I kept in the back of the classroom to ourselves, signing small phrases Cat taught us. Much to my knowledge, the Allies had no clue about the sudden shutdown. Cat was unable to reach the Homing Herd due to firewalls and new technological challenges. She said she would update us when she had the chance.

Regardless of what was to come, I made sure to feed her ideas by telling her about my latest discovery to speed up the process. Cat took notes as Kim said he would test it with his glasses.

"Great, this is what we need to move forward with our plan," Angela whispered to me over Coach Mike's screaming. "Find bags and start packing."

I gave her a thumbs up and returned my focus to Coach Mike.

By the time the day ended, I did as she said and found two bags in the closet of my supposed room. One bag for me and one for Max.

"What are you doing?" Max asked me as I stuffed several toiletries and a first aid kit into it.

"You'll see," I reply, afraid of saying it out loud. I'm positive they bugged this place. "Trust me on this." I place a single finger on my lips.

He stays quiet, and I continue to pack. Thankfully, I was able to find a loose floorboard large enough for me to place the backpacks under. When I'm done, I return to the living room and slouch on the couch with him, watching the TV.

He pulls out a notebook and a pencil. "Do this." Max lightly strokes the pencil over the paper various times. A few letters appear on it.

I take the notebook from him and repeat his motions. Bumps of the words he had previously written lightly bulge out of the paper, enough for me to read.

"How much longer?" It says.

I take the notebook writing a response, pressing the pencil deep enough for when I erase it, he would be able to read it.

He retrieves it and shades in the areas I wrote in. He bobs his head back and forth, putting the notebook down.

We exchanged a few times until the lead of the pencil broke. I take the shaded pieces of paper and drench them in water. When they were soaked enough, I shredded each piece of paper with my hands and threw it all into the sink's garbage disposal.

Satisfied, I sat back on the couch with Max, turning on the TV, searching for a specific episode of Steven the Dog.

"Wait, I liked that one." Max attempts to steal the remote from me.

"Let me play you an episode and then we can watch it." I scolded, holding the remote away from him.

He narrows his eyes and crosses his arms.

I click on the episode where Steven the Dog teaches us the basics of sign language.

I turn to Max and gesture to him to pay close attention, raising the volume of the TV. Together we practice with Steven the Dog until the episode finishes.

"Play it again," he tells me.

"What about the other episode?"

"I like this one." He replies, understanding my motive. We practice and practice for the days that follow.

Each day I made sure to inject myself with the serums I had stolen from Esmeralda. They did a number on me as I felt numb in the places I struck the needle. While it did hurt, it was worth it every time. I felt stronger as though my insides were made of iron metals and titanium. I didn't feel as defenseless as when I first arrived.

I tested my limits and tried to see if anything would happen to me if I did two at a time. I woke up with Charles carrying me, and my eyes turned green like the liquid. The effect wore off within hours. I kept telling myself "If it didn't kill me, I should be fine." like some kind of mad scientist, hungry to see what comes of me.

I became my very own experiment.

It was exhilarating and a total rush. No other medicine had given me the same effect as the serum did. I grew impatient whenever I ran out and purposefully hurt myself in the process. I was desperate to get more and was satisfied when I did. I stole continuously from the infirmary. Several nurses were willing to give me the serum as a whole to see what I would do with it. They knew me all too well by the numerous times I had come in after getting 'hurt'. They took notes and kept tabs on me as they never had a patient who had taken so many dosages as I had.

"I'm afraid you'll turn radioactive," Esmeralda tells me. She spotted me inside with a broken wrist. That time it was an accident. We were playing basketball, and I landed my knee on my wrist trying to get the basketball away from the opposing team.

"This is only my third dosage this week. The last two were given to me because my arm didn't heal well enough." I explained to her.

She saw past my half-lie and warned me about the consequences of addiction. Ironically enough, prior to my captivity, I never understood addicts. I was always puzzled by how often they consumed themselves with drugs and alcohol as if it were their life source. The way they shifted their demeanor and lost themselves under the influence, saying that it helped them. For a child, it didn't make sense.

Now it does.

I wish it didn't.

"You don't want to risk a heart attack, do you? And leave your poor brother here all alone?"

"No,"

"Then I suggest you stop whatever you're doing."

"Yes, Esmeralda."

"It's Ms. Esmeralda. " She corrects me.

After our interaction, I took her advice and slowly weaned myself off the serum, getting rid of them one at a time. It was an awful experience. I despised the cravings that would follow whenever I reached the bottom of the liquid. The adrenaline and rush I would get would fade into dullness, leaving me back into the shell of my body.

As I took the last batch of serums, I made sure to swiftly dispose of each needle as I flushed them down the toilets until there was none left. I had to be as discreet as possible.

The companions were very circumspect when it came to keeping us in line, unlike the nurses. It made me wonder if Esmeralda had talked to Charles when he wasn't busy chaperoning me. Their interactions suggest they had some sort of relationship going on.

Like Esmeralda, Charles also commented on my eyes. He found it odd when they didn't turn back to their normal brown. By my last dosage, it was apparent they were going to stay like that, a nice shade of olive green.

Max had a theory that it was because my genetics were finally kicking in.

"Why do yours look like that? It's nothing like mom's and I."

"Maybe it's because I had brown eyes, so my shade is darker."

He glances at me up and down with his pair, gawking at me.

"I don't like it."

As for the Allies, library meetings were practically non-existent as our companions had to be in the meeting room with us. Instead, we took it to the lunch tables as it was the one place where we could freely talk as the blaring speakers concealed our words, and it gave the Allies time to practice their signing with Cat.

It took several attempts, but we successfully made it through without using our words. I slowly began to improve, and so did Max. He told me he had shown Mika, and soon enough, she too would be up to our level.

Speaking of Cat, in the past couple of days since our last exam, she has managed to hack and locate shipments of what goes in and out of the facility. As for what happened during the lockdown during exams, there wasn't much she was able to report since she, and I quote, said "It's top secret".

I didn't question her any further given that I didn't want to risk any suspicions of possessing too much information. Instead, I focused on one thing and one thing only, preparing for the big escape.

I wasn't sure when it was going to happen, but I'm proud to say that I was prepared. The backpacks hidden under the floorboard were filled and ready for Max and me. I made sure we had enough to keep us alive.

I studied where we'd flee based on the small pieces of paper Cat slipped at the lunch tables. If you put the papers together, you'd be able to form a map she sketched out. It was vague as Cat said it was "too dangerous" to tell specifics. In the last escape Cat had planned with Kim, there was a snitch among them that foiled everything. (It's also the main reason why Kim wasn't against me joining. He opened up to me and told me he thought I would be the snitch of the group.) They were both lucky enough to not spill anything important such as the exact coordinates to the headquarters.

"Once we are out, you all must follow me, Kim, Xander, or Angela. We'll lead you to freedom," she said.

Having pieces of the map gave me the impression that she trusted me enough to find the route on my own without them if the occasion called for it. Based on what Cat filled me in on, we had to move for about three days until we got to our final destination, the sewers.

Everything was going into motion, and I slowly began to find myself as I no longer possessed any more serums.

A few days before the escape, I had an argument with Max. We were sitting in the living room, and I briefly mentioned the possibility of leaving the facility. He grew uneasy when I told him that the backpacks were ready.

"What if we stay here?"

"Don't you want to go home?" I ask in a low voice, making sure it is difficult to hear past the sounds of Steven the Dog.

I was still very wary about surveillance as I doubt there wasn't at least one bug in the room. Sure, you can call me paranoid, but I've learned the hard way to think twice before saying anything out loud. A boy in my history class was mauled not long ago because he said the word terrorism audibly. He was one of the few pinks left.

"I do," he replies, shrugging his shoulders and sinking into the couch.

I could tell there was something he wanted to say. He was simply afraid to tell me. There was a subtle tension within him as he moved the ball from his dominant hand to the other. It was a small gesture that told me everything I needed to know.

"But?"

"But it's nice and safe here. Our companions say the outside world is dangerous."

"The outside world? Dangerous?" I turn to him, scoffing in utter disbelief. I raise the volume of the TV in the living room. We watched the episode where Steven the Dog was breaking out of prison for a falsely accused crime. He used his super strength to bend the prison bars and reach his lair.

"Yes, dangerous. You saw what was happening on TV. The building was on fire, and people were screaming. Mom and Dad wouldn't let us play outside. We had to hide."

"We had to hide because of THEM!"

I couldn't believe the words he was saying. I was afraid he would succumb to their ideologies while we were here, it was only a matter of time. He's grown too comfortable with *them,* especially with his companion, Lori. He always spoke highly of her as though she was the sweetest person despite her attempt to attack me with her baton when he had been unconscious. I still had yet to tell him about the incident.

"Max here is where it's dangerous. Dangerous for ME." I insist, trying to keep my calm.

I had to convince Max to escape with me, otherwise, all this planning would be for nothing. I couldn't stand the idea of leaving him here. Either we both stay, or we both leave. End of story.

"El we have food, water, everything-"

"What about Mom and Dad? Huh? They're probably worried sick because we're in a place like this."

He remains silent, lowering his head to the ground. This incredibly annoyed me. He was so defiant with words yet cowardly hid behind actions like a fraidy cat. There was no medium whenever it came to his extremities or lack thereof. I wanted to scream at him and tell him to grow up. I am so exhausted from having to take the lead. He had one job, and it was to listen. Why couldn't he just do that?

"So, you think we're safe here?"

He nods his head hesitantly as though he is debating on his next course of action. Debating if it was worth fighting with me over what he wanted to say.

"Max, they're brainwashing you!" I say, having enough of his antics.

"No, you are!" He snaps defensively, stepping away from me, and replicating my outburst. His eyebrows arched, and his grip on the ball tightened. For once, he created a wall between us. The type of wall that only he could climb. I couldn't recognize him for a split second. He looked like one of *them*. He just needed the uniform. It triggered something in me.

"You want to play that game. Fine. We'll play that game." I narrow my eyes to him.

Perhaps I have sheltered him too much for him to face the reality of our situation. I thought by holding back the details, I was protecting him from trauma, but instead, it was leading him to deception.

"Do you know what happens to us when we fail those big kid exams?" I questioned him, turning up the television to its maximum volume. Sounds of the prison bars breaking intensified as Steven the Dog tried to break out of his cell.

"No-"

"I do. I watched it happen." My voice progressively raised. "I watched them get killed right in front of me! If I was a pink, I'd be dead Maxine! If I don't pass the next round of exams they give us, I will be gone. Forever. Do you think I feel safe? Do you think I want to

DIE here? LOOK AT ME!" I screamed at him as I ran my hands over my head, brushing across the bald exterior that once was covered in dark locks of who I was before. Feeling the sensation of emptiness was the final tumble. It opened a vast wave of emotions that took over my senses and minimized my patience.

I had enough.

Capturing his attention, his orbs snapped up to meet the absence of my hair. He finally was looking at me rather than around me. I could tell it pained him as he could no longer meet my gaze since the haircut. It affected him as it affected me. His grip on the ball intensified as the webbing of his veins appeared on the surface.

"Max!" I yelled louder, frustrated.

He keeps his head down, biting the side of his cheek and squeezing the ball.

Maybe I crossed the line.

"Answer me!"

"If…"

"IF WHAT!" Anger rose to my throat faster than I'd like it to. Both of my hands were at my sides in fists. My unclipped nails were the least of my concerns.

"If we leave, we can't leave her behind," he whispered finally.

Blinking, my lips parted open for the question to come out.

"Leave who behind?"

His lips open partially, and I ask again.

"Mika," he said finally. "We can't leave her. I want her to come with us."

There it was.

The truth spilled out to the floor for me to pick up. I became unsteady with what I had to work with.

I didn't need any words as he understood enough from the sigh that juggled within my head and heart.

It all made sense now. The reason he was hesitant to leave. I had completely forgotten about Mika. Maxine had a heart far too big to think selfishly as I do. Admittedly, it felt like another hassle on my plate, *another body to keep alive.* I felt guilty for thinking of her in such a way, but it couldn't be farther from the truth. Maxine alone was a handful.

Taking a deep breath, I crouch down on my knees and meet his stare. His cheeks turn pink, and his eyes water.

"Oh, Max." I brush away a tear from his face, fighting the urge to not allow myself to slip.

I can't afford to go soft now. Not as his sister. I reminded myself.

Right now, I am simply his guardian, and as such, it is up to me to lay down the reality of our situation. I couldn't tell him make-believe stories like I once did. This isn't a fairy tale anymore; it was simply a nightmare.

"No. Don't do that." He pulls away from my fingertips.

"I-"

"Promise me. Promise that when we escape, we'll take Mika with us." He cuts me off.

"Max-"

"Promise me!" He lifts his head and meets my gaze. There is an urgency in him that makes the veins in his eye pop. It reminded me of the exact look our mother made right before my head hit the floor.

It was moments like this that recalled that exact memory over and over again. What's snapping me out of it is my need to develop a proposal that can convince him to leave with me. If there's anything I have learned, it is that it is impossible to change the mind of a person lost in the haze of their goals.

It's a risk, but it's one that I will have to take.

"I promise," I say finally. "I'll pack her a backpack. I don't know how I'll do it, but we won't leave her. I'll make sure of it."

The corner of his lips turns upwards, and relief falls over him like rain in the desert. Each drop of hope was enough to keep the light in his eyes from fading into the darkness. Because I had lost my light, I was more than determined to preserve his. He is far too young and far too little of a child to fall into despair. I will turn myself into a net if that means he won't fall into the cracks.

21

They gave us another.

Another.

Damn.

Review.

Sheet.

Rage filled my heart as fear rushed towards my legs. There was no warning or preparation. They threw us into the lion's den with little to nothing for us to grapple with. The first review sheet hit me with a strike. The sensation felt like those needles I stabbed into myself except there was no high, only a deep low sinking feeling that left me discouraged.

The sensation worsened into a puncture when it was Ms. Charlotte's turn to cough over a study guide. She was overtly unbearable. Much more than the previous teachers that is. They were challenging to deal with but predictable. Meanwhile, Ms. Charlotte was a complete wildcard.

Her treatment towards us was far from endearing as she did not bother hiding her joy when we walked into her classroom. Her smile widened when she spotted a few sheets of our previous guides pinned to our clothes. She made an absolute effort to make a performance as she fanned the sheets of blinding white paper like dollar bills and selectively chose who would and wouldn't receive one.

"The youth is our future, and I will treat you all as such." she would say.

Treading in her six-inch heels, she cautiously weaves her way around the room grinning widely enough to make any court jester envious. She had a pattern to her behavior as her thick eyelashes moved a certain way to those she'd handed the study guide. By the time her footsteps crept beside my desk, her purple lipstick was smeared across the top half of her teeth.

She was far too gleeful for my liking.

Swaying her hips to the edge of my seat, she towers over me, leaning forward in close proximity to my face. Her breath reeked of alcohol and cigarettes. She attempted to hide the potent scent with layers of fragrances. It didn't work. The stench was strong enough to burn my nose hairs.

I kept my temptations to plug my nose seeing as she examined me with her orbs. They lowered and rose until she reached my shaved head. "You're usually a calm one," she tells me.

It was a statement. An open invitation to talk. A trap.

Luckily, I knew better. I don't open my mouth. I let her words bounce off of me, revealing little to no expression possible. She was waiting for a reaction, and I wasn't going to give it to her. She doesn't deserve it. After all, with the escape being so close, I had to be cautious and calculative. As long as I am here, she can do whatever she wants. She could kill me right now. But what's the fun in that?

No.

She liked playing games. That's who she is.

She analyzes her opponents, and when they're at their weakest, she goes straight to the throat. It's the reason why Mason lasted as long as he did. She liked having a victim, that is until she grew impatient. It was her fatal flaw. She lost her toy and craved a new one.

"I am quite surprised what has come of you. Clearly, you have potential, but whether it is good or bad is up to question." Her eyes lower to the bruises on my fingertips. I held onto my desk too fiercely. I should've planted the palm of my hands down on my lap. Maybe if I did, she wouldn't have the upper hand in noting my mettle.

One side of her mouth shapes into a snarl, captivated by her current findings. She pauses in her place, deciding on her next move. I erroneously lowered my head, allowing her to strike. She brushes her sharp talons across the center of my bare scalp, leaving small traces of blood and indentations on my skin. Traces of her.

She has marked me. I am next.

The best comparison I could give of the sensation is that of a chalkboard and nails. My bare scalp was the chalkboard, yet unlike it, I stayed resilient. I did not cry.

"Thanks for the massage, but your technique needs some work."

"Shut it!" She slams my head down and tilts it to its original place. She digs her nails further into me, inching closer to my skull. "I will give you one more chance. Go on. Say something. I'll make it your last."

She traces her claws further down, carving me like a pumpkin. A small drop of blood falls under my chin past my cerebral lobes. Fighting the urge to spin around, I sat there waiting. I waited in silence until she was done playing with me. Satisfied with her design, she gently placed my review on the desk right at the wooden swirl I forced myself to fixate on. Her nails were the color of blue skies blurred with my DNA.

"Good girl," she whispers, leaning down to me. "I see you, child. You remind me of myself. There's a spirit worth saving. If you continue to behave, I might spare you. Hell, if you make it past graduation, you might be lucky enough to have me as your mentor."

Never.

I keep my eyes open, biting the back of my teeth. I wouldn't let her get to me. Not while she was in control.

"Don't worry child. You'll see. Here, your ticket." She slams the study guide on my desk, spreading her fingers open. I flare my nose and remain still. Exactly how she wants me.

Pleased, her purple lips widened in approval. In her devil heels, wielding an imaginary pitchfork, she continues to the boy in front of me. For the remainder of the class, I kept my head down, concentrating on the wooden swirl at the center of my desk despite it being covered by the bloodied sheet of paper. It did its job of preventing me from losing my current composure.

Near the end, Xander shared his sympathies from the corner of the class as he marched over to me and wrote something directly on my study guide. I blinked at him as it was unexpected. He bid no mind to Ms. Charlotte as she was forced out of the classroom as the companions stormed in. If class had not ended, she would've punished Xander her own way.

Sitting up out of my seat, I read the words he wrote: "Meet me at the infirmary". The word infirmary was underlined three times.

I raise my eyebrow and hear the snaps of bone breaking as he fights his companion. He immediately calmed down when the damage was done. The two exit the classroom and in comes Charles among the other companions who came to pick us up.

"Take me to the infirmary" I order Charles. I raised my hand to my ear and dared to see how much of it would be stained. The wounds were still fresh along with the stinging sensation. She cut my scalp deep enough for it to potentially scar. Her nails were imperfectly sharp as a knife.

Charles ignores me and continues straight ahead until I smear some of it onto his hand.

"What the hel-"

He turns over to me and darts his gaze right at my hairless blood-filled sphere. The bottom of his crusted lip lowered to a faint gasp.

"What did you do?" He questions me accusingly.

"I didn't do anything. It was Ms. Charlotte who did this to me. I listened to you and made sure I wouldn't cause trouble. Here's the study guide if you want proof." I wave the sheet of paper in front of the two planets that are his eyes. Underneath them held deep wrinkles that continued to grow each time I saw him. It made me wonder how on earth these companions stay awake if they're always on patrol.

He snatches the sheet from my hands and returns it to me just as harshly. "Very well." is all he could say to me.

He turns on his heels and guides me in the opposite direction of the halls. Standing outside of one of the rooms is Xander's companion leaning against the walls smoking a cigarette. He didn't bother to hide his crime as he slouched deeper into the wall when we reached his proximity.

"You know the rules, you're not allowed to smoke in here," Charles asserts to Xander's companion.

The man chuckles and pulls out a lighter, igniting the cigarette once again. He blows the smoke out of his mouth towards Charles's face. "Don't make me laugh, I just got here, Charlie."

"It's Charles." his voice deepens.

"Whatever."

I let out a cough, exhaling the second-degree smoke. The companion laughs and blows another puff directly at me. The color of Charles's pigment changes into a stop sign.

"Inside." He orders with a stern voice.

"Huh?" I say, turning my head upwards to see who he is talking to. In the process, I noticed a small vein on his neck. It grew double the size and led towards the dark bags beneath the creases of his eyelids. I've seen Charles mad before, but nothing like this.

Thud.

Xander's companion hits the wall and around his neck is Charles's bulging fist.

His hands were on Xander's companion's neck.

Companions on the opposing side of the hall who were also waiting for their assigned child, slowly turned their heads, captivated by the tension. Xander's companion chuckles under Charles's choke hold, causing the cigarette to fall out of his mouth. It falls right beneath his boot, sizzling in defeat.

"Infirmary. Now."

"But-"

"NOW!"

Yikes.

Without seeking another warning, I comply and march through the double doors. I immediately spot Esmeralda in the far back of the room, attending to a small child hooked onto several monitors. The child was practically lifeless.

Sorrow flooded her optics as teardrops fell past her heart-shaped cheeks. Unable to part ways from the child she kisses their bloodied hands, closing her eyes tightly, and whispering a few words of sentiments. When she lifts her head to touch the child's cheek, the monitor shuts down next to them.

Simultaneously, the lights flicker and return to their normal state. The monitor stops functioning, and the child flees past me in her ghostly form. Audibly weeping, Esmeralda falls on her knees, covering her face.

She had lost her patient.

Several nurses march over to Esmeralda, tugging at her arms to get off the floor. "It's okay."

"It was her time."

"She was a troubled child."

One after another try to talk some sense into her, with urgency in their voices. Esmeralda shoves them away from her, with a sickened expression. It had "How could you?" written all over. She kicks at a cart and with her arm, knocks over the streamlined monitor.

SWOOSH!

An irked doctor enters the scene, ordering Esmeralda to control herself. "There's plenty of them." He says.

Mortified, fury washes over Esmeralda. She snatches a small scalpel from a tray and stabs it right in the doctor's eyes. He screams in agony, gesturing to the other nurses to stop watching him and help him. Esmeralda then proceeds to grab another utility I don't recognize and pins the doctor's shoulder to the solid marble floor.

"Come this way," a nurse says, stepping in front of my view. He ushers me to another part of the infirmary where more curtains hung from the ceiling.

Where is Xander?

Chills crept throughout my body. The monsters I had kept locked in the wrinkles of my cerebrum broke out of their cages. The curtains grew and the space around me condensed to the size of an elevator.

What's wrong with me?

I was fine until…. until….

"Agh!" I flinch when he nears the cotton ball to the slashes of my scalp.

"Hold still. Sit down." He orders, spouting more commands to me.

"Stop!" I screech, overstimulated. No more touching. I can't. Thorns. It feels like thorns.

"I said hold still!" The nurse roars over my protests.

Another nurse appears through the blue curtains. "What is going on?"

"She won't hold still!" He keeps his grip on me while the other nurse scurries for reinforcements. "What did you give her?"

"Nothing! Yolis! Franco! We need reinforcements."

Large shadows enter the enclosed space, pinning me down on the metal table.

The shrieks of a banshee escape my throat. Their hands. Their hands are all over me.

I blink back the clouds around my eyes, making out the figures hovering over my head.

"Ella. Hey, it's me." Another pair of hands touch the surface of my inflamed skin.

"Xander?"

"Kim. It's Kim." He heaves over the other figures underneath the blazing light.

"Where's Xander?" I sucked in a breath as the sedative disorientates the world around me.

Their grips around me loosen except for one on my left hand. Kim nods his head, and the male nurse quickly weaves in the remaining stitches, applying whatever remedies for a fast recovery. When he is finished, the nurse leaves my sight and leaves me alone with Kim.

"It's over." He tells me.

I squeezed my eyes shut, unable to stand the lighting. "Where's Xander?"

"He'll be in here soon."

"Why are you here?"

"They same reason you and Xander are."

I shift my head to the side, adjusting my eyes to the blur of the sedative. He had bandages covering the side of his rib cage. Tints of red crept through the white fabric leading me to believe the injury was deeper than I think it is. In the pocket of his pants, several bloodied study guides poke out.

"What happened?"

He leans in the cushioned chair, folding his arms. His tongue rolled from one side to his cheek onto the other, debating whether he should spare the details.

Recalling what I have heard across the halls, some had to fistfight for their study guides. There was one teacher who was known for that, though I didn't have him just yet. "Survival of the fittest" was his reasoning for everything, especially when figuring out who was "strong" and "smart" enough to solve his ridiculous math problems. He believed that those who could keep up with his equations were worthy of saving. The rest can rot for all he could care.

Putting the pieces together, I am led to believe that Kim may have had his class while Xander and I were with Ms. Charlotte. Granted, the teachers have been getting increasingly violent by the day. More kids are getting captured, and the classrooms are filled right back up again. As far as I am aware, we were at maximum capacity.

"We're moving the escape," he says instead of answering the question.

The lights flicker once again as though there was a power outage running through the building.

"To when?"

"Tonight."

Xander appears through the curtains with Cat and Angela behind him, both equally as injured. They held up their battered study guides. I pull mine out of my pocket crumbling it tightly.

"Good."

The lights go out completely. The monitors go out like crazy, and the nurses scramble rapidly in the darkness. The sides of our mouths widen, and together we lay out the final details.

II

The Escape

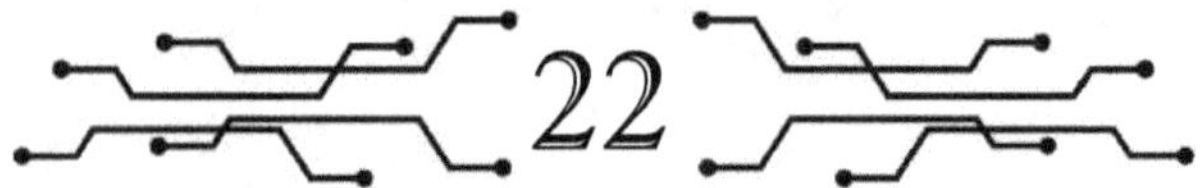

We had to move quickly.

It was obvious enough that every second counted for any escape. In a sense, it was like that one episode of Steven the Dog, Max, and I watched. Steven had to rescue his friends on an alien spaceship before the timer went off. On that timer was an electromagnetic bomb that would destroy the entire spacecraft and those in it. He skillfully finds his friends in time, minus one unlucky crew member who sacrifices himself to save Steven and all his friends.

Yet, unlike the cartoon, various lives were going to be lost. I wasn't stupid enough to allow my delusions to mix with fiction. This was our reality, and I have to treat it as such. Based on what we discussed in the infirmary, the Allies and I, along with the poor unknowing children of the facility, had less than twenty-four hours to get out of there alive. Panic was right around the corner next to Chaos. Potentially, among the table, serving a bone-chilling dessert is the Grim Reaper. His scythe was nicely sharpened.

I told myself it was for the best. He was going to arrive at the party anyway. It was only a matter of time. By escaping, I was giving us a second chance at life. It was the entire reason we *had* to leave. I couldn't allow myself to risk another chance of the flawed exams. Ms. Charlotte was set on her vendetta. If I acted as I pleased when she first provoked me, I would've been the first on her list. My name would be crossed out in red ink several times. Each line would signify a tally of times she would hit me with her ruler.

I touch my scalp, rubbing my fingers over the areas she clawed.

Speaking of the escape, there is one major detail I could not leave out of my plans. That detail is Cat had planned to shut down the entire facility for exactly five minutes.

That's all we had.

Five entire minutes.

In those five minutes, I had to:

- Get Max

-Find Mika

-Somehow get past all the companions that would surely try to keep us in with their weapons and electric batons.

-Get us past the barred fences.

Oh! And arguably most important of all, keep us from getting killed!

Easy peasy right?

Furthermore, from what Cat has told me, when the shutdown happens, there will be sirens ringing and our doors opening as they will unlock. Nothing can keep us in as long as the power remains off for those five minutes. That includes the elevators.

Having known the facility's inner workings over the last few weeks, as Allies, our objective is to herd as many of us as possible out of the facility and onto the forest grounds outside the barred fences. From there, we would have to run for our lives and survive for the next three days until we made it safely to one of the Homing Herd Headquarters. I knew only one of the headquarters, and plan to go to that one if I can't find Cat, Angela, Xander, or Kim in the dark.

That being said, during lunch, I made sure to snatch all the final snacks and pieces we would require for our three-day journey. I went as far as taking a few items out of the cabinets of the infirmary and stuffing them into my clothes. I had pills, clothes, and green-filled vaccines that made Max and I have those oddly super-strength abilities.

Concealing all the items hidden in my jumpsuit, I was more than eager for the day to end and to pack it all away into the backpacks I kept under the floorboard below my bed. Though I had one more task I had to do before midnight, I had to figure out how we'd be able to locate and find Mika in total darkness. The only idea I had was her tracker.

Ever since I told Cat about my discovery, the majority of allies have taken theirs down. We have gone unnoticed thanks to Cat's technological skills.

"Given that we do the same things every day, I have calibrated our trackers to replicate our previous steps. They'll never notice a thing." she signs mischievously.

Luckily, I had forgotten to dismantle Mika's tracker.

When the day was coming to a close, I stuck around with Mika and Max during dinner time while the Allies informed the others of the grand escape tonight. We couldn't afford to do it any other day as they pushed for exams to be tomorrow. The blues were next.

"Mika. When the lights flash red, and your door opens, I want you to run to the courtyard. Don't be frightened when that happens. Okay. Everything will go smoothly as long as you find us there. Do you understand me?"

If the tracker were to shut off during the outage, I at least had a designated place for me to find Mika. I was ready for any and all of my tactics to fail. It is how I always managed to get away with my schemes during elementary, such as by seating myself next to Rebecca during tests to copy off her. If I was feeling extra crass, I would arrive at school extra early to obtain access to an empty classroom. The teacher and I would converse until they left to use the restroom. I would go over to their desk and glimpse at the answer sheet in the drawer of the teacher's desk. It worked a handful of times, and not once had I been caught.

Those tactics seemed small in the grand scheme of things. This time I have to make sure I left no premise untouched.

She bobs her head, shifting the position of her headphones.

"Make sure you take those with you too." I lightly tap on them.

She nods her head once again, turning over to Maxine for approval. He agrees with my plan and clenches the baseball in his other hand, careful not to burst its seams.

I may not have been able to tell them everything, but they knew enough for us to be okay. They are smart kids, and as long as Mika follows her orders, Max will too. I had to believe in them, otherwise, it would all fall apart.

I will get them out of here. If I had to be a human shield to get them to the other side, then so be it.

Calculating the seconds that have gone by during dinner, the time ticks closer to midnight. I know of this when the companions storm in. According to my estimation, approximately three hours were remaining.

As I instructed, Mika distracted her companion so I may swoop in to grab one of their holotablets. She ran in circles, giggling and laughing until the device finally slipped out of their pocket. Before it could hit the ground, I carefully caught the tablet and slid it into my jumpsuit. It slides past my chest and remains stuck at the waistband hugging my hips. Ignoring its cooling sensation, I nonchalantly cross my arms, hiding its irregular shape. It worked too well as the companions lost their suspicions during the examination period.

"It's a study guide." is what they likely assume. They gave up on patting us down as they knew what was coming for the blues. It didn't matter how hard we studied, in the end, we'd be like the pinks, non-existent. Of, course, there is the rare bunch that survived based on their talents.

"The smartest and the strongest of them survived." Kim stipulated.

As the metal doors open again, and I am greeted with the wooden scent of our living room, a pleasing satisfaction fills me with joy. Present in my chest is the holotablet. The device was under my control.

I did it!

I carefully turned it on in the bathroom, pressing the applications of the tablet one by one. One app, in particular, displayed a three-dimensional outline of the entire facility. It was the same app Cat and Kim had used that one time in the Allies meeting. Pinching the screen with my fingers, I was able to locate and zoom in through all the possible staircases and exits I could find. I navigated through the diagram as though I were crafting spells in the air, twisting and turning my hands quickly to examine each corner of the facility. Sadly enough, the projection did not display the area outside of the barred fences. I was hoping it would give me an idea of where to go, but hey, it's better than nothing at all.

In another application, I was able to locate every child in the facility. Each child had a profile image and depiction of their color and name. I put Mika Alden into the search bar, and like magic, her location appeared on the screen. I tapped her profile two more times to spy on her movements off of the tablet. She was located precisely three floors below us.

If anything, she would be the first to make it out to the courtyard, which would give me the advantage of quickly spotting her and weaving our way out to the forest. It was only a matter of time and patience.

Patience.

Like a lioness, I needed the patience to hide among the fields until I was ready to strike. I can't be too early, otherwise my prey will get away, and I will be left sitting there all hungry with vexation.

"Do you need help?" Max asks, hovering over my shoulder as I scurry in the halls.

"No, but if you'd like, you can take this." I give Max his backpack and allow him to add anything else he wants to take with him; such as the Steven the Dog blanket I had in my room. I was surprised by how he was able to make it without the zipper bursting. When we were both set, he curled on the edge of the couch, and I permitted myself one last trip to the bathroom.

I wanted to take a good look at the girl on the other side of the mirror before I left her there forever. She wasn't going to come back. Not until we were safe.

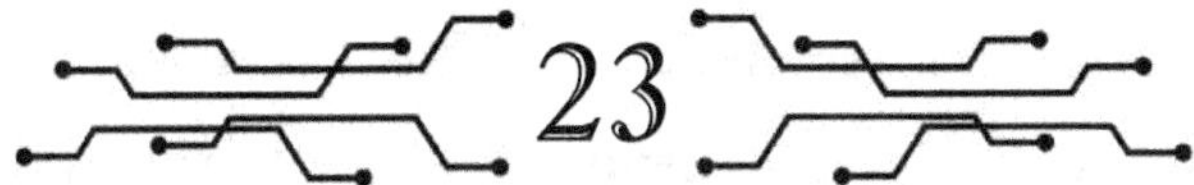

Crossing her arms and leaning against the wall, her dark locks of curly hair cascaded brightly. It extended past her shoulders and perfectly bounced at her waist, tidy. With a lack of excitement, she expressed her internal turmoil, cursing harsh words at me.

How nice.

"I'm sorry," I whisper, taking a step closer to her. I flickered my gaze to sink as I skimmed past her narrowed eyes.

We didn't bother with introductions. She knew what was coming the second I laid my eyes on her. She wasn't ready. No one ever is.

"You're not sorry. You know exactly what you're doing here." She taps the mirror with the tip of her finger accusingly. I twist the side handle, unleashing the valve. It felt like I was turning on a switch inside of me.

"Hey!" she slams the mirror, with her pristine fists. "Look at me."

I reel my whites to her, trespassing her defenses with great intended aggravation. Like a small rabbit, she jumps away from the mirror, mystified. "Oh no. No. No. I didn't mean it! I've overstepped the line. I see that now."

Woosh.

Woosh.

Splash.

The water ran like the sands of an hourglass, measuring the time she had left. Small specs of her ran at the tips of my fingers as I checked underneath the spout to see if it was warm. Boiling hot was how I liked it.

"You don't have to do this. We can still be together," she helplessly negotiates.

"No, we can't." I surmise, as I dove into the avalanche.

"Please."

"I've made my decision." I sigh. "I'll make sure it's painless."

"Painless?" She freezes in her place, scanning each and every bruise on my body. She presumed that's how I was going to leave her.

With the lavender-scented bar of soap, I clean my hands, scrubbing them to their purest state. Though, they won't be like this for long. She knew this. She'll be the first to stain them.

It's for the best.

I didn't want her to be there during the massacre that was going to occur in the next couple of hours. The things I am willing to do and have braced myself for would go against all her morals and everything she stood for. By hurting her, I was also protecting her. To me, it was easier to let her go while she still had an innocent soul; one of us had to have one.

I was doing both of us a favor.

Splashing around, as she stood there, fixated on me, we couldn't help but compare one another. She wore confidence like a sweater, while I wore a vest of determination. She colored the world around her while I ensured it stayed black and white. She loved her every being, while I craved to find any notion, I liked about myself.

I was completely stripped of her, minus one factor. Our dedication to keep everything together. We were equally quizzically observant. Every detail we micro-analyzed during our time in the facility had never fled our minds, and in the process, perfected our tactics to stay out of trouble. To protect Max. To become unstoppable.

Taking the first shot, I run my hand through my head, and she does the same. Except, a clump of hair falls past her fingertips. Panic sets in, and she repeats the process until she ends up like me. Her eyes widen in horror, and a smirk plants on my lips.

"My hair!" she cries.

Dropping down, she scrambles on the tiled floors, attempting to pick up the few strands she could find.

"They'll never catch us now," I whisper. "It made us weak. Vulnerable. Tangible."

"Make it stop!"

I wipe my wet hands over my blue clothes as if they had her blood on them.

"Don't you see? This is why I can't keep you. You wouldn't survive. But I, *I will*."

Cupping the strands, she eyes me with such disgust. As if we weren't the same.

"You're a monster!"

"Maybe, but I won't let you last long enough to see."

I place my palms on the counter, reaching for the weapon.

"Wait." she pleaded. Seeing as there was no means to get through to me, she picked her last moment's treasuring bits of herself. She caressed the curly strands, weeping like a child as she alternated with every curl.

When I am done watching my latest spectacle, I grab the hairbrush she once used and smash her out of my sight. Glass covers the bathroom, falling into pieces on the ground. Very few cut my skin.

An unfamiliar laugh escapes my lips. It was that of a shriek and a deep chuckle combined.

Plunk!

I peer at the tip of my toe, and seize an elongated shard, measuring it with motivation. I wield it in the air and rub my thumb across the edge, testing its sharpness. I knew what exactly to use it for.

I leave the bathroom and sit next to Maxine on the couch with the backpacks right at our sides. Despite the anticipation, we somehow fall asleep, listening to the static of the television, and waiting for the ghoulish sirens to sing their song.

24

Right on cue, they sang.

As Cat had promised, they woke Max and me from our nap. Flashes of red covered the room as the metal doors went out.

"Hurry!" I yelled over the alarm.

We lift ourselves out of the couch, removing the trackers on our ankles. I tugged Max headfirst to the darkened halls and joined in among the buffalo stampede. Like a monkey, Max clung to my body while I maneuvered us to the passageway of emancipation. A few disorientated companions got on their feet and attempted to haul us back in, but there were far too many of us to let that happen.

"What are they going to do? Give us detention?" I overheard as a pink fights off their companion using a pen he held. He stabs the companion over and over until he grows limp. I yield Maxine in front of me and point in a direction to distract him.

"Everyone remain in your rooms!" The voice shouts over the sirens. "Escapees will suffer the consequences!"

Like a tsunami, companions pour into the halls with electric batons at their sides and masks across their faces. I recognize the gas tanks at their hips and instruct Maxine to put his on. It was one of the last-minute supplies I'd obtained in the infirmary. You can never be too prepared. These sick murderers will do anything to keep us hostage.

"Max, whatever you do, don't look behind you!" I yell through the mask and over the sirens, tightening my grip on his small hand, in fear that I'll lose him among the children around us. We were packed together in the halls like wild sardines, mushing and running up against each other for any passageways out of the facility. I held Max more intensely when I spotted a small child trampled on the ground on the side of the walls. An older brother grabbed the child and threw him over his shoulder, maneuvering out like the rest of us. I disregarded shock and decided to put the holotablet back into the pocket of my jumpsuit as it acted more of a hindrance to carry. Instead, I swap it for another item.

As we make certain turns (most of which I had planned when I was studying the facility), companions around the perimeter start to use their batons, pounding and electrocuting runaways. Those with the tanks at their hips released their potent gas, causing my fellow comrades to drop like flies. It was a quick and efficient tactic as a few of the companions were already tossing their little lifeless bodies back into their cells.

I quickened my pace as these hospital masks were going to last us for so long. Like a holy grail, out of the rat maze, I found my gateway. Right in front of me are two large metal doors that should reveal a pair of long staircases that lead to the courtyard. Standing on the opposite end of the handle stood a soldier with an electric baton, grinning ear to ear.

"Got you," he says, swinging the baton towards my head.

Pulling Max down with me, I ducked past the swing and pulled the broken shard of glass, I had replaced the holotablet with. Using every strength I had in my arm, I sliced through the companion's neck, screaming at Max to close his eyes. Flashes of red lights among the sirens covered his cries and bits of his face.

As though it was a scene pulled right out of a slasher film our parents used to watch, the companion bled out and, in the process, stumbled backward past the railing, falling into the depths of the staircase.

I hover over to see if he has survived the fall.

He did not.

There on his neck is the silver shard I had stabbed into him.

Hearing others pour out the door behind us, I tug Max's frozen body down the stairs. He couldn't look at me. Not in the sense that he couldn't make eye contact, but rather he couldn't look at me as the person I am now.

He searched for his sister.

His Elena.

The girl I left back in the mirror.

"Hurry." is all I could say, keeping my eyes forward, making sure not to trip over the steps. It was a long way down, and we had too little room for error.

He follows my heels with slight hesitation. In response, I curl my pinkie over his and he rushes faster to my side. After what felt like an eternity, we eventually made it down to the last floor, fumbling to avoid the companion's body as the shard grazed my ankle.

How many minutes are left?

For good measure, I rip the baton out of his dead hands while we are still inside, and hand over the bloodied shard to Max. He grimaces at the sight and refuses to take it from my hands. Rather than start another argument, I drop the shard and keep the baton on me. We used its flashlight feature and guided ourselves deeper into the outskirts of the building.

Spotting an exit, we open the doors and hear a few others enter the staircase as their steps pounded loudly one after another. Some of them sound like children, and some sound like companions. I didn't dare look back as I was afraid if I did, I might lose hope.

I slam the last door open and green the outdoors with open arms. It returns the gesture as a kiss of a breeze coaxed our skin, producing a small cloud out of our mouths. Hundreds of kids ran past us speeding through the red flashing lights and flailing their arms in the open air. They all scattered among the barred fences and fled with injuries beyond repair.

"Where's Mika?" Max asks, scanning the crowd from where we stood. He held Mika's backpack, picturing her in it.

"We have to keep moving." I urge him.

"Not without Mika! You promise!" he shouts.

A sharp pain hits my eyes as the watch towers turn on and shine their lights over the thousands of us who made it outside. I vigorously type in the holotablet, ignoring the helicopter swaying ahead of us.

On the holotablet, Mika's dot glows from the center of the courtyard, and my stomach drops. Max releases my grip and runs straight into the swarm of people. I yell his name and attempt to follow after him. A girl not much older than I am shoves me down and forces me to the ground, losing my place. Various feet trample over the holotablet I dropped, breaking it into pieces.

Oh, shoot.

Covering my head, I lift myself away from the mob and scan the crowd for him. In the corner of my eye, I notice the soldiers in the watch towers loading in the ammo while those ahead of me slide under the barbed wire through a hole that had been dug. I see Xander guiding them quickly and pointing in the direction of the forest. He doesn't seem to notice me.

I have to find Max. I remind myself.

Running out of time as the power began to return, I climbed over the side of a nearby watch tower, clinging onto the sides. A companion climbs after me and I swing the baton right at his head. I must've used too much force considering that the baton broke in half, and he flew off the tower. Above us, helicopters swoop in closer aiming their weapons at the center of the courtyard, placing the spotlight directly on Max and Mika.

"Run!" I shriek to them as bullets rained from the sky.

Max turns and grabs Mika in the direction I pointed to as heavy metal rained from the skies. Dancing through shadows and flashing red lights, I witnessed the banshees soar as they were set free from the lifeless bodies that once were filled with childhood spirits. They begged me to survive and escape their fate.

I obediently listened.

I quickly climbed down the tower and using the strength and speed I had developed over the past few days, I ran past those bullets they were shooting overhead. Most had hit those around me as I felt their bodies underneath me.

Their bodies were so small.

So squishy underneath my shoes.

My blood-stained blue shoes.

I saw their banshees everywhere taking the forms of their bodies, floating off to the heavens above where they were no longer bound by the facilities. They waved at me each time I passed by their corpse. One body in particular that caught my eye was that of Bea. The bullet went directly into one ear and out the other. I let out a gasp and forced myself to keep running. From afar, I found hope as I saw that Mika and Max had made it to the barbed wire. They were covered in mud and wore the backpacks I had packed for them.

They weren't dead.

I sped faster than ever, feeling the lights on my skin. The bullets kept on going, tracing my footprints. One hit my heel as my fingers touched the outer wire.

I mutter a curse word under my breath and fall flat on my face.

"Elena! Get up!" Max shouted at me from the other side gesturing to me to run faster. Along with him and Mika, Xander stood near the barbed wire, peeling it open for me to crawl to him.

"Hurry!" He pleads.

BANG!

BANG!

BANG!

One after another bullets strike behind me as I roll my body over to the opening. Two kids who were at least three feet away from me got hit and collapsed at my sides, dead.

I was the last one.

"Shit" I curse, feeling the wire tug on my backpack. There was still a bit of a distance to get to them.

"Leave it!"

"No, If I take this off, those bullets will hit me-" Preceding my warning a single bullet hits close to my chin.

"Go." I insisted as I struggled to keep my head down.

"But-"

"Listen to your sister! Go! I'll stay with her!" Xander snaps at them for me. Max frowns and passes his cat eyes over me. I hold up my pinkie and flick my finger.

"GO MAXINE!" I order. He flinches with a pained expression and runs into the forest with Mika.

I dig my arms down and like a turtle, I slowly move from my shell and through the wires to reach Xander.

"SOLDIERS!" A voice thunders from afar. It resumes through the speakers ordering the others to run inside. They lower their weapons and stop shooting at us. A few more soldiers and nurses stay on the basketball courts, mindlessly piling the bodies into large waste bins. They were outrageously nonchalant. They disregarded the bodies with little to no reaction or courtesy. One nurse kicks a boy wearing purple into a bin like a soccer ball. She grows frustrated when his body doesn't move the way she expected it to.

They were nothing to them.

Their names.

Their faces.

Their lives.

They only saw us as objects—colors to be exact. We were to be disregarded whenever we didn't follow their stupid rules and their stupid expectations. That's why they got rid of the majority of the pinks. Only the smartest and most talented ones survived.

"All staff must seek shelter. I repeat seek shelter." The commander mandates over the megaphones of the watch towers. In unison, the soldiers and nurses leave the bodies in a singular pile and retreat to the inner workings of the facility.

Xander and I glance at each other with uncertainty, thankful for the peace yet terrified of what is coming. They were merciless. We both knew that. They weren't stopping without the last lick.

"Just go!"

"No. We have a chance to leave, now hurry up."

Leaving the backpack, I break free from the wires and catch Xander's hand from the other end. He pulls me out from below and we both smile at each other. I keep my grip on his hand, tugging him gleefully.

We made it.

"Come on." I rejoice as we step into the forest. When we made a fair amount of distance, I called out to Max and Mika wondering where they were. Without the light coming out of the facility, it was difficult to see where we were going. Footprints were practically nonexistent as the pitch-black mud sloshed the soles of our sneakers.

Out of nowhere, when we reach a clear opening, Xander stops in his tracks gaping his mouth open in horror. I follow his pupils, expecting the worst.

A helicopter swings from above, dropping a large explosive right at the center of the courtyard we had just left and another several feet in front of us. Within seconds a gust of wind and balls of flames collide against the leaves as Xander covers me with his entire body, recognizing the bomb before it hits the soil. Smoke filled the air and just like that, my smile fell. His mouth was moving, and I couldn't hear him. I couldn't hear his voice over the ringing in my ears.

It hurt. Everything around us hurt and was filled with smoke.

I could barely breathe. Like snowflakes, ashes covered the skies, dusting Xander and I. He moves his mouth again in the same motion. I understood one phrase, "Elena".

My name against his lips.

I hated myself for understanding that singular phrase. Heaven knows what else he said while his body was sizzling on top of mine. His lips moved with urgency as if he wanted me to hear his last words, knowing that I would be the only one to be his witness. He takes a sharp breath and tightens his grip as another bomb goes off. The ground shakes and his head drops over to my shoulder.

We had to keep moving.

"Xander," I say softly, feeling the weight of his stoic body underneath the rubble. "Come on. We have to go. We need to leave."

I turned his body away from mine, lifting myself out of the ground to face him directly. With the palms of my hands, I cup his face, hoping he'd react in some way. Not a single movement was detected. His mouth lingered on words he had spoken last, and his eyes stayed open and still. Those eyes, those wonderful brown eyes against his translucent skin. I thought he was pale as a ghost when I initially met him, but now my worst imagination has come to fruition. He became a ghost. There was nothing inside the shell of his charred skin. Absolutely nothing.

"We were supposed to make it! Look! We're out of the facility." I choke, hopelessly gesturing to the path we came from.

Another bomb goes off in the other direction, thundering with vengeance. I hold him tighter and he doesn't flinch. "Xander please," I beg, rubbing off the mud covering him, only it wasn't mud.

"Oh god." I clasp my hand around my mouth and wrap my hand around my waist, holding myself up. I stayed that way for what felt like an eternity until a snap from a twig forced me back to my feet.

"El." says the voice.

The bombings became louder and more prominent. I turn to the voice and see Max and Mika hiding behind a tree. They were covered in ash and blood, none of which was their own.

"We hid in a small ditch. Mika got scared and so we went looking for you." Max murmurs.

His eyes then lingered over to Xander who remained still. Another bomb goes off and he flinches, placing his hands over his ears. It was another reminder of my duty. Max and Mika were my priorities.

Pursing my lips, I kneel over Xander checking his pulse, and squeeze his hand once more for good measure. There was nothing more I could do. We had to go. We had to leave Xander and make our way to the headquarters while we still had the chance.

I had to leave him. Leave him here alone in the darkened forest with nothing to protect him.

I had to.

I knew he wasn't alive, yet a part of me couldn't process how he was gone within seconds. How he had simply said my name with such vitalness. How it all fell apart so quickly.

"I promise you, I'll make it out alive. For the both of us." I vow, curling my pinkie over his and snapping my finger in the air. I let out a sigh when his hand fell and forced myself to stay composed. I pretend to be like Steven the Dog and carry on with my mission as he always does and like him, by the end of the episode, we will be happy and at home.

"Let's go."

I turn over to my heels facing my back against Xander. I take his untouched backpack and wear it as mine. I pushed all my emotions below and flicked myself out of the girl I left in the mirror. There was no time for her compassion. I told myself that she had to go…at least until we reached the headquarters.

Another bomb goes off and I pull Max and Mika away from him.

"What about him?" Max asks tearfully. Thankfully it was dark enough to only make out his shape. Mika and Max had seen enough for today.

I shake my head and swiftly reply "He won't be coming." I glimpse over the trail Xander, and I came from, reflecting on how much more we had to go. I swallowed back the lump in my throat and took a shaky breath.

Max closes his mouth and I pull them deeper into the forest together, following remnants of the map in memory. The leaves sizzled into crisps of emptiness and the winds howled all night long. I listened to every bit of nature's sorrows, making sure we'd make it far enough to leave the ashes past us. There was no stopping now. Not when the darkness was on our side tonight.

We were going to make it to the headquarters one way or another.

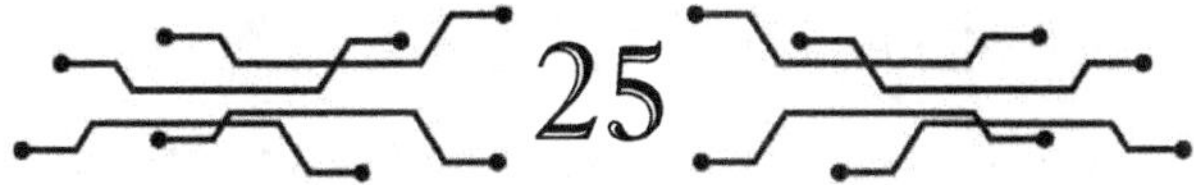

We traveled through the forest until sundown, or at least what we believed was sundown beneath the smoke covering the skies. Grey and black tinted the earth along with the freshness of the forest air. It plugged my sinuses and irritated the open wounds on my flesh. The earth beneath our feet shook and we kept on walking. It eventually stopped as we reached a small stream where we could drink water after traveling for so long.

Relief washed over me as it verified my internal navigation.

"Follow the ways of the water, and soon enough, you'll be at one of the headquarters," Kim said right after Cat provided me subtle details of the HQ between our conversations during lunch. He would then resume going back to his plate of food, poking and prodding.

I instructed Max and Mika to refill their water bottles and let them be in the meantime. They obeyed and left me to take care of the rest.

Using what we had, I've cunningly set up a nice camp for us for us to relax. I took the liberty to lay out our equipment while Max and Mika slept under a pile of leaves, I compiled together into a makeshift bed. It was far too hot to be bundled up, so they used the Steven the Dog blanket as a pillow. I almost woke them when I accidentally scared myself during my rinse in the river. It took me a minute to realize that the bleeding was normal, though, it became yet another hassle for me to deal with. I had to create sanitary napkins out of the leftover toilet paper we had and make the most out of the ache in my abdomen. I was thankful my mother had educated me on this particular subject as I would've completely lost it if I hadn't known what to do.

While I was at it, I tended my wounds with bandages I've kept and injected myself with one of the remaining serums where the bullet hit my foot. I waited for it to set in and dried myself completely when I was done with rinsing out my potential infections. In the process, I somehow found the audacity and the courage to go through Xander's survival bag for an extra pair of clothes considering I no longer had mine.

To my surprise, I found more than I expected. Inside were letters and a small, loaded gun. The letters were addressed to his family and the core members of the Allies. I quickly set aside the weapon and turned to the letters.

His handwriting was blocky yet legible like graffiti and ironically enough, read like classic poetry based on the several details he portrayed and the expansive vocabulary he used to describe his surroundings.

In those letters, he wrote about his experience inside the facility and how he planned to find them once he got out. I was teary-eyed when he wrote to his deceased sister as it was filled with missed memories and apologies. They were emotionally strenuous to get through knowing he was no longer alive to deliver these letters to them. The more recently dated letters took me through several emotions as he wrote about how he met Angela and how she helped him to establish a newfound friendship with the others.

I stopped reading them when I reached the mention of my name. While I was curious about what he thought of me, I had too much respect to let myself read that far.

It felt invasive. *Very hypocritical of me, I know.*

Here I was rummaging through his backpack and reading his personal letters, and I drew the line at my name. My stupid name.

"Elena," he said among other things while the bombings went off and my ears were utterly useless.

I felt shameful.

These were *his* things before I took them. The extra clean oversized clothes were *his*. The snacks I ate were *his*. The flint and steel I somehow found among the pockets and used to make a fire were *his*. He had enough items to survive if he wanted to.

Xander vaguely mentioned to me how his family came to Crinx United to get away from the war. It was evident he knew exactly what he was doing and knew how to survive because of his past experience. He wasted his precious life saving mine. He should've guided Max and Mika to the HQ, not me.

Exasperated, I snatched a rock beside me and tossed it straight into the river. "Ugh!"

Under the tree, Max shifts in his sleep, turning over to the side. It was a reminder that I still had obligations to meet. Moping around and hating myself wasn't going to do a single thing.

It wasn't going to bring Xander back.

I placed all the letters back into the small pocket of the backpack I found them in and prepared myself to catch our dinner for the night.

It took a few trials, but I caught a few using the palm of my hands. Most of it had to do with patience, which I clearly didn't have. Max woke up laughing when he spotted me splashing around the shallow end of the river strangling a floppy fish that escaped my grip and slipped into my lap. At this point, I was drenched in water and shivering from head to toe. The river water, while amazing to drink, was cold to the touch.

I snatched the fish by the end of its tail and skewered it with a pair of scissors I had packed inside Max's backpack.

"Gross!" Max exclaims, recoiling away from me. "Please tell me we are not eating that."

"Yes, we are. If you could give me a hand, that would be wonderful." I reply, passing the scissors to him so that he can cook them by the fire. He gags and resentfully takes our dinner from me.

"Gracias."

He shoots me another glare and turns the fish to the other side. Mika, oddly enough, volunteers to help me. Without having to ask, she removes her shoes and enters the water. A small noise comes from her ankle, and I quickly toss her back to the dirt. Max drops the food and turns over to us concerned.

"What's wrong?"

The noise grows louder and the device buzzes on her ankle.

"The tracker." God, how did I forget to deactivate hers."

"Is everything going to be okay?" Max shrinks back, applying pressure to the baseball in his other hand.

Mika shakes, placing her fists on the sides of her head. She mumbles incoherent words over and over.

"Mika stay still," I ordered her. I swiftly place both palms at the sides of the tracker and grip it with my thumb and pointer finger. Using every ounce of strength, I pry the damn thing open. In the process, flashes of black and white explode until I let go of the device on her ankle.

I fall on my back wheezing in between breaths, allowing the grass to stroke my skin. "Mika, are you okay?" I murmur.

No response comes out of her mouth.

"Mika," I repeat.

"She's okay," Max answers for her. He cradles Mika in his arms, but she is quick to push him away. Instead, she rolled around in the grass next to me until all her senses reached equilibrium.

I let her calm herself down and explained to Max that she was overstimulated and needed space. After surviving electrocution, I wouldn't blame her if she didn't want anyone to touch her for a while. Especially since I was still able to feel a slight tingle on my fingertips.

All those injections were worth the pain.

Because of the green serum, I had thus far been able to survive past bullets and break off the tracker like never before.

The tracker.

Picking up the two halves, I couldn't help but worry. What if they already know where we are? What if Cat or the others forgot to turn off the trackers of the escapees? More importantly, how long do we have until they make their way to our location?

"What's going to happen?"

"Nothing. We're leaving."

"Now?"

"Now," I say scrambling to pack our backpacks. They act quickly without hesitation and follow my lead. I defuse our fire and stare at the trees, judging the light bouncing past the remnants of the horizon, debating on how much time we had left until it was dark. Thankfully, there was a fish fully cooked for Mika and Max to munch on while we walked. They complained on the way, begging me to carry one of them at a time for each mile we met. I complied considering they didn't weigh as much as I expected. The hardest part was ignoring the sting of their arms wrapping around the exposed areas of my burns. Max and Mika suffered less considering their injuries were cuts and bruises.

Along the way, we made a short stop for a potty break. Mika found a berry bush and plucked one for me to taste test. They stared at me intently as I swallowed the berry. It was not poisonous.

When I nodded in approval, they feasted on the bush. There were a few times I had to reprimand them for slowing down as every movement of the light mattered. The sun became my timekeeper. Soon enough, when all there was shadows, I permitted us to stop completely and rest. This time we made sure no traces could be detected.

I monitored the levels of the streams, examining how wide it had become throughout our travels. I could only assume more fish were swimming in it.

That's a good sign.

The more fish there is, the more we can eat. For extra care, I set aside a small muffin and an orange for Mika and Maxine to eat for breakfast, in case they got impatient in the morning. A breeze passes the night and the two shiver. I pull the Steven the Dog blanket out of Max's backpack and drape it over them.

"Wake me up if you guys hear anything at all. We will be leaving here once the sun rises." I yawn. "Do you understand?"

They obediently bob their heads and situate themselves for our slumber. In the silence, river water felt like an ocean and cricket noises became a concert to our ears.

"Good," I mumble, blowing out a small twig I had lit when it had gone dark.

I fall to a patch of grass, spreading myself like butter. My feet burned in pain along with the rest of my body. I knew I was sore, but as I was resting, I found the extent of my injuries. There was nothing but skin and bones in me. Because of the tracker incident, I had nothing left in my body. I took the chance to eat a cricket that happened to encounter my body while I attempted to fight the sandman.

I didn't want to sleep. Every time I closed my eyes, all I could picture was the worst. My worries were the best craft for nightmares. There wasn't one scenario where I couldn't imagine being caught by the G.C.P.O.A.

They had trucks, we had our feet. They had weapons, I had my bare hands. It felt like a losing game. I won't relax until we make it to the headquarters.

"El," Max whispered. "Are you awake?"I move my eyes away from the blurred constellations and turn to him. "Did you hear something?"

He shakes his head, rustling the leaves under him. "We can't sleep. Do you think you could tell us a story?"

"Maxine."

"You said you'll tell me a story someday. You pinkie promised."

"And you want it to be tonight?"

"Yes."

"Will you two sleep if I do?"

"Yes." They both reply. It felt nice hearing Mika's voice. It was as soft as a rose petal.

"Very well. Hmm, let's see." I pause, thinking of what I could possibly come up with. To be frank, I had forgotten about promised his story. I was a tad too busy on our escape to have anything prepared. Heck, the planning and plotting seemed easier than squeezing out the last bits of creativity I had left.

"Any day now," he yawns.

"Okay, okay. I think I got it. Once upon a time-"

"How original."

"Do you want a story or not?" I snap.

"Yes," he mumbles. Mika chuckles and waves her hand telling me to continue.

"Ahem, once upon a time, there was a brave soldier. Her name was…" I bite my lip, thinking of a unique name for me to give.

"River," Max suggests.

"River! Perfect! River was the best soldier ever. She fought away thousands of monsters."

"What kinds of monsters?" Maxine inquires.

"Tons of different monsters. Tall ones. Hairy ones. Monsters big and small. River fought them all to save her kingdom, Oplius from doom. By her side were her two pet dragons, Nelly and Midnight."

In the story, River fights against an evil Vampire King named Scolim. Using her special magical sword, River protects her people from the Vampire King by slicing off his hand. The Vampire King grows angry and leaves the village.

"Is that the end?"

"Not quite. You see, while the Vampire King fled from the Kingdom, he spent those years in the shadows coming up with his revenge."

The shadows of the fire grow bigger adding a fear factor to my story. Maxine and Mika shrink in their clothes and wait for me to continue.

"On one unfaithful day, while River is out searching the forest for food, Scolim sneaks into the Kingdom unnoticed and strikes again, only this time he comes after River's dragons."

I pretended to snatch something in front of them like I was Scolim.

Mika and Max jump back in unison with wide eyes.

"Upon their capture, Nelly strikes the vampire in an attempt to protect herself and her fellow sister dragon, Midnight. The Vampire masterfully bites Nelly, sucking out the life of the first dragon. Nelly dies and the Vampire grows stronger."

"Oh no." Max gasps.

"He then approaches the second dragon, widening its sharp fangs." I widen my mouth open, bearing my teeth to them. "Right before the Vampire could take its first bite, River swoops in to save the day. She swings her sword of steel and slices the head off of the Vampire." I slice my neck with my hand and pretend to be dead.

"Together, Midnight and River save the town once more and live happily ever after. They no longer had to be afraid of any monsters or evil Vampires."

"That's a terrible story!" Max exclaims, throwing his hands in the air.

"And why is that?"

"What about Nelly?" Max questions, crossing his arms defensively. Mika raises an eyebrow and stares at me keenly.

"She's gone. Sometimes a sacrifice happens when you want to protect someone. Because she sacrificed herself, she successfully managed to protect and keep Midnight alive." I reply. "It's like the one episode in Steven the Dog. Remember when his friend Luke the Dalmatian escorted everyone out of the enemy spaceship and stayed back with the enemy to make sure the bomb took them all out?"

"Yeah."

"It's like that." I reason. "Without Luke's sacrifice and bravery to help those people out of the spaceship, none of them would've made it out alive. It had to be done. There was no time, and someone needed to stay behind to be certain that the bad guys stayed dead."

"I see." Max yawns. "Is that why Luke was happy when the bomb was about to go off and had told Steven he'd see him on the other side? When they meet up in heaven?"

"Yes," I reply, expecting him to ask various difficult questions regarding life and death. They weren't the most facile concepts for him to comprehend.

My family and I learned it the hard way when he accidentally stepped on our hamster, Sherman. On one unfaithful morning, Mom was cleaning Sherman's cage and forgot to lock him up in a safe place. By the time his cage was clean, he was already gone. Mom did her best not to panic and spent all morning looking for him until it was time to pick us up from school. On the drive home, she explained to Maxine and me the unfortunate news of our beloved hamster. We both grew worried and made a pack to find him. Maxine was far too eager, and in the act of running around the house, he stepped on the poor little guy. He picked his hamster right up and showed him to me with excitement.

"El, look! I found him!" he jumps, waving the dead hamster right in my face. I tell him to stop moving and to hand Sherman over to me. When he did, I screamed. My parents scurried to us and saw what had happened to Sherman. We try to explain to Maxine that he is dead.

"No, he's not." He shouts defensively.

"Yes, he is! You killed him! You killed Sherman!" I retaliated, cupping the hamster in the palm of my hands.

After we buried him in our backyard underneath the fig tree, my parents had to hold us back from fighting. We shouted at each other from our rooms for weeks before we started to calm down. After we got along, my father sat Maxine down and explained the logistics of death using the newest (at the time) space episode of Steven the Dog. Max grew silent and moved on. Back then we didn't know if he understood or not.

I still couldn't tell.

Maxine doesn't say anything for a while. Instead, he stays still, gazing at the same constellations searching for Luke somewhere amid the galaxy. Mika points at her favorite ones and I give her a brief explanation of its shape and what it means. I told them everything they needed to know about the stars and their stories. This worked a lot better than the tale I made up for them. They found comfort in my voice, and in a sense, I too became lost in awe. It lasted for what felt like hours until they fell under the spell of the Sandman.

Still restless, I kept myself occupied by counting the stars and listening to the roars of the river. I guess I could say the beauty of darkness was how it made me notice the world a little more. Every little shift in the waves and glow of the stars muzzled into my memory. When I felt ready to be dusted, I closed my eyes and dove headfirst into the sand.

That night, I dreamt of Xander.

26

I found him by the river, basking in the horizon sitting down in the grass with his feet dangling over the deep ends of the river. He patted the space next to him and I obliged. He was dressed in white robes as if he came down from heaven itself and held a letter in his hand. He seemed at ease, peaceful even.

We shared a couple of words of sentiments and played with the river water until all that was left were us and the stars. His white clothes progressively grew stains of soot and the scars on his body became prominent. A knot twists in my stomach knowing the limitations of our time together.

I didn't want to let this moment go.

I felt safe. Happy. Content. I went as far as allowing myself to forget Max and Mika. My hair grew longer, and I was a kid once more.

"Xander?"

"Yes?"

"Remember that time at the library, when you asked me who my favorite poet was?"

"Mhm."

"Well, I read your letters…which I'm sorry for doing by the way, but um… I just wanted to say."

I anxiously curl my fingers into fists. "I wanted to say that you'remyfavoritepoet."

He chuckles lightly and keeps his gaze in the distance.

"I love your metaphors, and the way you write about everything with such symbolism. It's so detailed despite the little time you had to write them. I saw the fingerprints and scribbles of where you rushed to finish the last sentences."

"I'm glad."

"That I read your letters?"

"I'm glad someone loved what I wrote." He clarifies contently. The breeze hits us a little more harshly as it removes bits of the hair out of my head. I was slowly back to the other part of me.

"Already?"

"Yes." He murmurs with a sympathetic smile. He takes my fingertips, squeezing it slightly. Flashes of when the bomb had hit us flood my vision, giving me one conclusion.

"It's a dream," I tell myself.

The world spins and changes into mayhem. The river waters turn dark and the grass bursts into flames. I touch the hues of red and orange, allowing them to engulf my fingers where Xander had touched. There was no burning sensation, instead, the coldness of the brisk winds of the night struck my skin.

The world shook a second time causing me to fall on my feet. Towering over me is the girl from the mirror, telling me to not lose hope. She hands me clumps of her hair to give me something tangible.

How could she be so kind to me after what I did to her?

As I reach for it, a voice thunders from the skies and the rest becomes hazy.

"ELENA GET UP!" Max screams, grabbing me with his strong hand. He forces me to lift from the ground and tosses me against a tree inches away from the stream.

Splinters cover my clothes and the sun peeps through my eyelids. "Max, what the hell!" I curse at him. My migraine returns with an extra punch.

I hold myself up against the tree with one hand and recenter myself. I had to rub my eyes with the other to see him underneath all the mucus around the corners of my eyelashes.

"Sorry!" He blurts, tightening his grip on the baseball. "I can't find Mika."

"She might've gone to use the restroom. Did you try calling out her name?" I suggest as I tug my neck downward to examine his face. His cheeks were puffy and red as though he had cried.

"How long has she been gone?"

"I-I-I don't know. Maybe thirty minutes or so? When I woke up, she was gone."

I curse under my breath and instruct him to grab our bags. "No matter what happens, I want you to find Mika and follow the river. I'll find you guys eventually, just don't stop moving."

He tugs on his backpack, nodding his head. I pat his back and just like that we dove headfirst into the depths of the forest. It was difficult to see where she could've gone as there were little to no traces of her to be seen.

"She couldn't have gotten far," I say aloud for Max to hear. He doesn't say anything. Instead, he squeezes the baseball and scans the potential pathways. We did this for quite a while until Max came up with a brilliant idea.

"Ella, pull me up."

"I am not carrying you right now."

"I mean up the tree." He rolls his eyes and points at a sturdy tree with plenty of branches for him to hang on.

I naturally fold my fingers together and boost his leg. He makes it the first try and lifts himself over a branch like he used to back home.

Funny enough, we were essentially built like monkeys. Mom didn't want us to build a tree house so Max and I improvised with our imagination and climbed the tree like a jungle gym. Mom hated it at first, but she eventually didn't mind it as much when we helped her pluck out the unreachable fig she wanted at the very top of the tree. We'd swing ourselves around and occasionally use it as our hiding spot when one of us got in trouble. One winter, we got banned from climbing the tree because Max slipped off one of the branches which resulted in a concussion.

Mom gave us a Spanish earful and ordered dad to trim the trees the very next day. When she wasn't home, we'd climb the tree and continue with our travesuras.

"Do you see anything?" I shout as he maneuvers his way upwards. Covering my voice is a thunderous gunshot. A scream then followed.

Max freezes in place, hugging the tree's trunk. "Mika!"

BAM!

Another gunshot thunders, causing the crows to fly out of their nest. They squawk their foreboding calls below. Like the ashes, black feathers fall from the sky and dust the trees.

"Max stay here," I yell, sprinting to the screams. They were prominent but difficult to follow as I wasn't sure which direction the echoes came from.

I yell Mika's name and find myself standing over a fresh footprint. They trail into a narrow rocky pathway where shrubs and tall boulders rub against each other. A small hill provided some oversight inside the opening.

Mika's cries grow louder, and I become resistant to my best judgment. Rather than climb the peak of the hill, I drive through the closing of the boulders and follow the footprints. To my dismay, I find Mika bound up and gagged. There were two other children chained up next to each other with lifeless eyes and bullet holes right in the center of their foreheads.

I let out a gasp, stepping back. A hand wraps around my mouth and waist. I thrash like crazy, fighting their grip. Mika wails in her bindings, struggling to reach me.

"Not another word or she will be next." The G.C.P.O.A. officer whispers. She holds a loaded gun to my head and clicks on metal cuffs with the other.

"Move," she demands, chaining me down next to Mika. She keeps the gun to my head and pulls out a small communication device. "Caught another one of these brats. Over."

"Do not act against them unless you need to. Backup is coming. Over." The voice responds over the static. The woman tucks away her device and kneels to me, snickering pridefully.

I wait for her to lower the gun at me, but she doesn't. She keeps the barrel steady at my head. I think of ways to distract her, but nothing surfaces. She was waiting for me to give her a 'reason' to shoot me. I'm sure of it.

Minutes pass by and she gets annoyed. She lowers the gun to my chin and reaches for the communication device, annoyed. "I'm getting impatient. Over," she grumbles to it. Nothing but static spews out of the device.

"I'm getting impatient! Over!" She slams the device on a boulder and repeats her phrase. She eventually gives up and finally lowers her weapon. "Heed to my warning, if you two attempt to leave while I'm gone, I will make no hesitation to shoot you. Understand?"

We remain perfectly still.

She lifts the gun to the sky and shoots it into the air.

"Do you understand?" she shouts. A small piece of food is stuck on her canines.

Mika and I muffle "Yes." under our gags.

She flashes her teeth and turns her back on us. As she does, out of nowhere a bullet rings and she falls to the side, slamming her head on a sharp rock. I followed where the bullet came from and spotted Max on top of the hill. He was using the gun Xander had packed. I guess we were in such a hurry that our backpacks got switched around.

Applying pressure on my wrist, I break out of the restraints and in the process set Mika free. "Come on." I tug her small hand. She remains still, frozen in fear.

"Mika, please."

She crouches to the floor, trembling and hitting her head with her hands. I bend down to her level and have her arms wrap around my body. Thankfully, she doesn't fight me back.

"Meet us at the river!" I yell over to Max. He signals a thumbs up and together we rush to our main location. I ran as best as I could, for us to get there. Mika's little hands tightened whenever I had sudden bursts of energy.

Max spots us at the edge of the river and waves his hands in the air. He points behind me and my adrenaline spikes to the clouds. A bullet flies past my ears and hits the tree next to me. Mika tenses and crouches her head deeper in my back. I let out a curse and ran without turning my head around.

I sped faster and instructed them to go into the river's waters once we reached next to Max. He switches backpacks with me, and Mika grabs hers.

"HURRY!" I urged, sensing them a few blocks from where we were standing. "Swim in the direction of the current, it is our greatest chance of survival."

Another bullet hits close and we dive our heads into the icy waters. Hypothermia was the least of our problems. The river was deeper than I expected. It reminded me of when I had attended Camp Wallby where we would have swimming races to see who was the fastest swimmer in our bunk. In the younger division, Max ranked in third place. I ranked in fifth place out of twenty of us.

I had hope for us.

In between strokes, I made sure Mika could keep up as she wasn't the fastest. I pushed her in front of me when I felt another bullet had reached the waters. One hits slightly above my ankle near the other bullet wound I had at my heel. I fought back a wince of pain and forced us to keep moving. The waves quickened and the river grew wider.

From the corner of my eyes, I spot figures emerging out of the piles of leaves and bushes. Scurrying in them were shadows of numerous officers loading their ammunition and aiming right at us with their overtly large weapons. I could tell they were struggling to obey orders as they hesitated in their aim. They easily could've shot me in the head if they wanted to. They had the right equipment for that.

"Keep kicking and spreading your arms. Don't forget to-"

I am cut off in the middle of my sentence when I spot a familiar object launching out the sky, directly above us. Grabbing Max and Mika by the shoulders, I pull them underwater with me, sinking them as far as I can go. The bomb goes off and all is disarray.

I open my mouth, to let out any noise for them to hear as the waters push us around in a frenzy, causing them to slip out of my grip. I flail around, attempting to have them in my reach. Instead, all I felt were the air bubbles surrounding my body. I attempt to open my eyes but become troubled when there is no silhouette in sight beneath the blur of the waves.

Unable to keep the air in my lungs, I resurface out of the water. I gasp for air and scan for their heads. Several bullets fall from the sky and soar past me, following the current.

I hear my name, and another bomb hits the water. The waves grow stronger and angrier than before. They roar into my ears and throw another mass flood for me to face. I slip under and crash my arms and legs into sharp rocks and large masses of fallen branches. I caught a small hand and they pulled me somewhat to the edge, overlooking the waterfall below us.

"Mika?" I blink through the harsh splashes of rushing waters. They bounce around like a hive of wasps.

We were both clinging off of a fallen tree she caught herself on. The tree was sturdy enough to keep us dangling, though, it was a matter of how long. It shook each time a powerful force made its way, causing the branch to swing us closer to the edge. It was evident that the bombs had angered the river as it woke it from its casual slumber. The river spoke in tongues of vengeance, making it difficult to keep ourselves dry. Another wave hits and crashes us with sharp leaves, trees, twigs, and several other objects. They scrape our sides and fall into the abyss or as I would like to say, the monster's mouth.

Among the objects, in the flicker of the moment, I spot Max sliding past me. I extend my legs out to him like a vine. He catches my foot with one hand and lets out a cry when swings himself in the open air.

The branch grumbles and faintly snaps, lowering us further to the depths of the waterfall. Mika shrieks and tugs her body closer to the tree with her one-hand grip.

"Keep on going!" I belted past the roars of the water monster.

She makes a second attempt, and the bark bends further. Like a faucet, water pours down my back and directly onto Max. His grip loosens on my ankle and Mika slumps in her reach.

"Not strong." She whimpers the two words.

Another wave hits and the branch bends further, leaving little to no opportunity for us to mess up the third time around. We have but a few moments left until the next tide hits and breaks the branch completely. We were running out of time and attempts. If we do fall, there's a chance Hell will be at the bottom. Of course, there is a small survival rate if it isn't as bad as I presume. There was too much water to tell, it was a fifty-fifty percent chance.

"Max, I want you to climb me and hold onto Mika."

"No."

"What do you mean no?"

"I know what you're planning. I don't want to do it."

"Max!"

"No! I don't want you to die! I pinkie promised you that we'd be fine. That you'd be by my side, and we'd be alright."

"Max, we don't have time for this. I want you to climb me and to hold onto Mika instead. When I let go, you two should be able to-"

"NO!" He shouts. His grip loosens, and I flash my eyes at him, peering at my bloodied ankle. I blink past the splashes of water hitting me all at once.

"Maxine! Don't you dare let go!"

"I'm sorry."

He peers up at me with those cat eyes of his. Except he was no longer a little kitten, he grew up to be a brave strong panther. Nevertheless, I still wanted to protect him despite his efforts to be heroic. At the end of the day, he's my little brother. He's all I have left.

He glances over to Mika who whimpers for him to hold on. The corners of Max's mouth tug into a sad smile. "Take care of Mika for me."

"Don't-"

Right then and there, as if he was preparing to fall into an inferno, he closes his eyes and releases my ankle. I scream his name and fall after him, letting go of Mika's small trembling hand. I hear her shriek loudly over the echoes of the roaring waters like never before. Her voice slowly fades all at once, and I am lost in the waterfall. I reach out in the midst of it all, in hopes that I could somehow grab Max and use my body like a cushion. The same way Xander had saved me.

It all was a sick cycle.

Upon impact as my body crashed into the beast's mouth, I felt a gravitational pull, sinking me further down its throat. I swerved and kicked as hard as I could to stop it from engulfing me completely. Out of nowhere, another body falls close to mine, creating another division of bubbles. I widen my view and pull my hand into the bubbles, grabbing the figure inside of it. We both emerge out of the monster's mouth, gasping for air.

The rays of sunshine blinded me instantaneously, forcing me to blink several times for my eyes to adjust. Swimming in front of me was Mika. She moves one of the pigtails blocking her eyes to the side and follows my lead in the waters.

On the outskirts of the plunge pool is Max trying to get himself onto a patch of dry land. He looked like he was struggling to maneuver himself as he angrily splashed his fist. He doesn't notice us until we swim to his side. To my dismay, the water was partially stained a dark red.

He bites the side of his mouth and tucks his head defeated. Above us, at the side of the waterfall, we hear several noises of soldiers rushing over. They were coming in hot.

Mika and I trade glances, sharing the same idea. We pick up Maxine at opposite ends and rush under the hidden crevices of the forest. I tell her to watch him while I keep an eye out.

I slowly weave my way from them and spot them from a trusted tree with an abundance of bushes for me to hide in. "Please don't find us," I whisper.

They stood over the waterfall for what felt like hours.

Searching. Waiting. Prowling like a pack of wolves. Who knows where exactly their loyalties lie to end up where they are now. I couldn't understand how an adult, especially an officer, could bring themselves to hunt and kill kids for a living.

Harmless kids.

Heaven forbid we try to escape our playtime with death while they sit back and choose which lifeline to cut.

I pulled the weapon out of my pocket and checked how many rounds were left. I scoffed when I realized there weren't enough bullets in the gun to take down more than a handful of them. I put them back, and re-load the weapon. It brought back memories of when we went to the shooting range. My parents wanted to educate us on gun safety. They would rather we be exposed to the weapon than to be blindly unaware of its usage and capabilities. Where we lived, as sad as it is, there have been a few incidents where people have been shot. We kept a single gun in the house if we ever needed to use it.

Of course, it was never within arm's reach of Max and me.

BAM!

One soldier points his gun at the bloodied waters and shoots at the area repeatedly. They must've believed we were still swimming in it somehow.

Making sure we wouldn't survive. The others did the same and threw their hand-held explosive below. While I was a fair distance away, I clasped my hands over my ears and ducked into the bushes until it had stopped. The ringing in my left ear persisted until it couldn't make any noise. When I checked again, they had turned away, following the direction of the commander. They all rush over excitedly, recoiling and reloading their large weapons. I waited until their presence felt inaudible.

Looking back, I wanted to kick myself for letting myself wait that long. Had I known what little time I was going to have with Maxine, I would've never left him and Mika alone in the forest.

I should've stayed with them rather than keeping watch.

I should've protected him better.

I should've been more observant.

I should've-

"Elena!" his voice groans impatiently. I wondered how many times he needed to call me for me to hear. It sounded muffled as my left ear slowly gave out.

At the time, I didn't know any better.

"I'm here Maxine! Don't worry!"

I spun on my heels and sprinted to where I had left them. Max didn't look well. He was losing color, and the puddle of blood grew. He was laid down with his head on Mika's lap. She wept silently and moved aside as I kneeled closer to him. I attempt to examine the wound on his abdomen while he squirms and groans in pain.

"Mika, I need Maxine's backpack."

I unbuttoned his jumpsuit and found several bullet holes around the same area. I could recognize that sterling silver anywhere. It was exactly like the one that came out of my shoulder. The same color, shape, everything.

I forced myself out of my flashback to focus on the present. I couldn't freeze up on him now.

Mika runs back to the plunge pool and snatches up the bags we took off of him. She returns with the bag, shivering.

I pour out its contents and try to wrap his abdomen with the Steven the Dog blanket he brought.

"I want to go to sleep." He murmurs, breathlessly. In my lap, I notice where his eyes are pointed. They extend over to the starless skies and great beyond. I wave my hand vigorously to keep his consciousness at bay.

"No no no, Max, look at me Look at me, *please*," I beg, pressing my icy-cold hands at the sides of his cheeks. "Mírame Maxine!"

He blinks a couple of times, trembling vigorously with each uneasy breath. Mika stood next to me with tears pouring out of her eyes. Cooling winds sweep through the forest, whispering their early condolences. I was completely in denial. I didn't want to give up my hopes when we had made it so far into our journey.

"El," He whispered as crimson liquids seeped outside the corners of his mouth with each cough he made. "Are they gone?"

"They're gone, Max. Everything is going to be okay. We need to go a little further." I cup my hand a little tighter around where he had been shot. I thought that if I applied pressure, it would save him.

> ***It should save him, right?***
> ***That's what they told me!***
> ***It should save him!***

We learned this at camp together. Our objective was to practice chest compressions on the dummy and build a tourniquet using the items they provided. I didn't do well, as Max kept me distracted. He kept on wanting to draw on the stupid dummy with his new expensive markers. At the time, all I could make out was the importance of putting pressure so that the blood could clot, which then somehow involved the tourniquet to stop the bleeding. I missed out on the last part because we ended up in the camp infirmary that night. Max and I both fell and scraped our arms and legs when I tackled Max to get the markers away from him.

Given the current circumstances, I wish I had paid better attention to the lesson and ignored Max. I should've just let him draw all over the dummy. Maybe then I could've done something to stop his bleeding.

A leaf falls from the tree we are under and cuts my cheek. The winds picked up, ready to collect its newest banshee.

"El, I'm scared." His mouth quivers and his body lurches.

"Hold on, Maxine. We're almost there. We're so close."

No, we weren't.

We had at least another day or so of travel left.

"I'm sorry," he cries, bouncing his head back. "I didn't want to slow you guys down."

"Shhh. It's okay. Look at me, Max."

"I don't want to do this anymore."

"No, no, don't close your eyes. Keep them open. KEEP THEM OPEN MAXINE!"

"It hurts." He sucks in a breath. "I want to go to sleep. Tell me a story."

I bite the side of my cheek, weighing my response. "Max, right now is not the time. I need you to stay awake," I murmur, pressing his wound as if I were keeping him together like a bag of liquid with a hole poked through. His blood soaks most of the blanket and past my fingers. It was enough to make an aspiring painter beg.

"Elena,"

"No!"

"It's like that one episode in Steven the Dog, right?"

"No, it's not. That's a cartoon-"

"El!"

"NO!"

"I'm going to die."

It wasn't a question or a statement. It was a fact. He knew, and I knew.

His eyes linger over to Mika and then back to mine. I could feel his pinkie inching over mine, his other hand holding onto the ball for dear life.

His favorite baseball.

I continued to hold on to him, drenched from head to toe in water and blood. None of it was enough to cleanse away our wounds. *His wounds.*

"My bag." My eyes widen as I instruct Mika to take mine off of me.

Like the other backpack, I dunk all the supplies out to the ground. Most of it was useless as it was drenched. The serums I had saved for the trip were completely shattered. The needles were bent, and the bottles spilled all over the insides of the bag. I rub my hands over it and apply it to Max's wound.

It did absolutely nothing.

His lips turn blue, and his eyes dilate in one place. I follow his gaze and notice a small bird in the lower half of the neighboring trees. It looked like a small dragon, but the size of a bird. I've only ever seen them in picture books. Max and I had tried to find them when we were out camping, trying to locate all types of species we could find. It was odd to see this little guy, especially in the biome we are in. From what I knew, to me, that bird was an indicator of how far we were from home.

"Nelly." He musters, smiling softly. "I see Nelly."

It was a nightjar.

"Max, I-" I pause, choosing my words carefully.

I didn't have the heart to deny his delusions.

"I think you're right. It's Nelly. She's gonna make sure you're going to the right place, okay? Follow Nelly no matter what. Pinkie promise?" I force myself to smile.

He nods slowly and I curl my pinkie finger without pulling away to do our usual finger snap. I was afraid if I did, I wouldn't hear a sound back.

His eyes well up in tears and so does mine. I brush them away from his face. Watching the bird with him, Mika scoots next to me and places her small hand over his chest. She twists her pointer fingers together, signing "friend". His smile widens. He kept his eyes on the bird until there was nothing left for him to live for. I realized this when his pinkie loosened its hold from mine.

His eyes stopped shifting and his body grew weak. "Maxine!" I shrilled, shaking his body vigorously. Both of his hands fall to his side, including his pinkie and his prized baseball.

Thud!

There it went and hit the ground.

I didn't think there could be a noise worse than bullets, but this one killed me. His body goes limp, and the ball rolls farther from Mika and me. For any normal person, the distance was only a few inches. As for me, it felt like it traveled miles away; unreachable.

It gave me nothing but one conclusion.

My brother was gone.

I had to bury his body.

He deserved at least that. I didn't want him to leave him like I did with Xander. It still haunted me to think about what the companions might have done to Xander's corpse by the time they found him. They probably shot extra bullets into him and tossed his body inside a garbage bag with the others who were lost that night. It was an awful thought, but it was realistic.

I wasn't going to allow that to happen to Maxine. If I leave him, I want to do it when I am at peace with where he is. It didn't matter how, I just needed it to be done.

Carrying his body on my back, Mika and I went the extra mile and found the perfect spot for him. The spot was located a few feet within the forest, surrounded by towering trees and welcoming creatures. There were rays of blinding sunlight hitting a small patch of grass, perfect for him to lie on. We measured the outline of his small body and spent hours digging until we couldn't anymore. It became my remedy for my anguish as I ripped apart each section of the earth, grunting and muttering curses under my breath. Mika pretended not to hear me.

In the process, a section of my nail came off and the rest of me was covered in mud. It wasn't much but we dug enough to cover his body. Mostly I did the digging as I occupied Mika with the task of scavenging for flowers mid-way.

She picked the best ones.

They were dainty and small like her. She also went ahead and picked a few mushrooms. Max would've loved them. I only wish I could've made him look more presentable to the eye as Mika them into the palm of his hands. He looked quite disheveled. Examining him from a living-dead perspective, I couldn't help but notice everything I had ignored before. He had scrapes on his chin and moss clouding his darkened hair. It made him look like a tiny woodland fae.

At the roof of his smile, a few of his baby teeth were missing and started to grow out of his gums. I felt guilty for not noticing sooner. I would've put a small item under his pillow so that he believed the tooth fairy was still visiting him despite being in the facility.

Present at the corner of his ear was a small cut trailing down to the side of his cheek. It seemed fresh.

Most likely he got it from when he fell down the waterfall or during the rush of bombs and water rapids. Following the rest of his body, he had various shades of bruises such as green, blue, and purple. There were the occasional misquote bites, but they were hardly visible in comparison to everything else.

I made a slight effort by closing his eyes and neatly wiping off the blood leaking at the corner of his lips. I then removed the Steven the Dog blanket from his injury and draped it over his body as though I was tucking him in for his nap.

His very long nap.

After we did our best to make Max shine, we stood over the grave in silence to bask in his final details before we were ready to bury the rest of him. Mika encouraged me to say a few final words as she signed a few of her own to Maxine. When it was my turn, I completely became stumped.

I was never really good with them. Usually, it was Max who was the talker between us despite being shy. After all, once you got him to speak, there was no turning off his motor. I thought about all of the things I could say to him, but none of them felt as prominent as the cafeteria chant. For some odd reason, that's all I could come up with in the grand scheme of things. I decided to follow it but with my own little twist.

"His name is Maxine.
Mighty and free.

His name is Maxine
and his blood stained like ink."

Mika repeats after me and waits for me to think of the next line. I proudly smile at her and continue.

"Our lives should matter,
and our people were shattered."

Together we repeat the remainder of the chant exactly like the day of the massacre.

"You have ruined our trust,
And this system is unjust.

We will shout and scream,
As we are human as we can be.

We say this a couple of times while we bury Maxine together. He slowly grew out of our sight as we covered him with more dirt. This process felt more difficult than digging his grave. The more I covered him, the further he felt from my reach. It's like he was fading away into the center of the earth. Mika felt the same as she burst into tears when she reluctantly held the final patch of dirt to pour on his grave. Her small hands returned to their trembling state, causing the pile of dirt to scatter around her.

"Max," she says with melancholy.

Hearing his name out of her mouth felt unusual, yet like a blanket, it gave me some comfort. It felt less lonesome.

I tightly purse my lips and nod my head. I lean to the side, cupping two piles for us to toss. It took every ounce of my sanity to bite back a sob. I had to keep my poise next to her. If she had to be strong, so do I. I admired her for being able to hold it all in up to this point. She was such a brave little girl. I don't think I would be as strong as her if I were in her shoes, especially at her age.

If I were her, I'd thrash on the ground, hyperventilating and screaming curses to the skies. I'd scream until I died of heartbreak, hoping I would meet Maxine on the other side. Part of me wants to do that now.

Together, we count to three and toss the last batch. It flies into the air like confetti and lands right at the center of his grave. I took the baseball Maxine had dropped and tuck it into the pocket of Xander's jumpsuit. I debated on whether I should've buried him with it or not, but part of me couldn't let go.

Yes, I know it was selfish of me. Sue me for all I care. There's nothing else left to take from me. That I knew. His backpack was practically extra weight, and there was nothing as equally as sentimental for me to keep. If the G.C.P.O.A. wanted it, they can have it. They can take their stupid backpack. They already took everything else. My home. My parents. My friends.

Added to the list was my best friend.

My brother, Maxine.

My brother.

I lost my brother.

I wished I cherished him more.

I didn't say it enough. I never got the chance to tell him. Tell him that all those nights I spent cheering him on at his baseball game were my favorite. That he was the reason why I'm alive. That he always made me happy. That no matter what he did, I could never hate him. That I loved him.

Despite our age gap, we were practically conjoined twins. Everywhere I went, he followed. If one of us got hurt, the other was there to help. We went through everything together.

For god sake, all I wanted to do was protect him! To keep him safe. That was my job as his big sister. Big sisters were supposed to scare away the monsters out of the closet and be the shoulder to cry on. It was *my* responsibility to keep an eye on him while we were away from our parents.

I failed. Terribly.

They say promises were meant to be broken, but I don't think this one was one of those. We were supposed to make it out alive.

I pinkie promised.

If I could trade my life for his I would. A cheesy saying, but it holds true.

I kept replaying all the things I could've done differently, but in the end, it was all the same conclusion. Those bullets couldn't have been avoided. Sure, if it hadn't been for Mika being here, but who am I to blame another child?

As the sun went down, Mika and I met eye to eye and decided to set up our camp close to the waterfall. Neither of us appeared to be in the mood to travel further into the forest given our exhausted emotional state.

I did my part by jumping back into the pool of water and catching a few fish for Mika and me to eat. The water lost its redness yet kept its chilling state, especially around my dirty fingers. They trembled vigorously in the water. I fought my shivers as my hunger was much stronger. Every time a fish was in the right position, I forced myself to dive underwater despite the terrible cooling sensation that would pierce my skin. I skewered a few and was thankful I didn't need to cook them. Mika was there ready with a blazing flame. She was a smart girl and a good survivor.

Using the branches around us, she hung our clothes to dry and kept an eye out for the remaining food supply we had left. Between the two of us, there was still a bit of snacks unscathed for us to live off for the next few days of travel, a handful of them were Maxine's. His loss also gave us an extra water bottle to reuse for our portable water supply.

We peacefully ate our kebabs and carried on with our day doing small but helpful tasks to keep us busy. Eventually, it grew too dark for us to do anything so we spent it watching the fire. I became lost in the flames as I debated on whether we should stay here or move on with our plans tomorrow. To me, leaving felt like the right decision, but the most draining.

All I wanted to do was lie on my back and listen to the cricket's symphonies playing in the shadows while I drifted into despair. Mika lies close to me and hums a song. I didn't disturb her, in fear if I did, something might happen. I haven't been able to have one peaceful day since everything has started. I wanted the world to stop turning and stay still where we are.

If I simply closed my eyes tightly and let my imagination stir, I would be able to pretend I was lying in the hammock strung by my favorite fig tree. The crickets sang like the ones by my bedroom window.

In that fantasy, I am safe.

We'd all be together in my backyard having a barbecue and chasing each other until the stars realign to whether they are currently.

Mika taps my shoulder and abruptly wakes me from my daydream. I spun on my heels to see where the danger was located. She tugs my arm and tells me to stop moving. My heart was racing like crazy.

She points at a specific place in the stars and traces its shape. "Nelly," she says. She traced the same spot over and over until I could somewhat see an outline. I froze in my place as the waterfall spilled onto my cheeks. A small lump built its way to my throat, stopping me from audibly crying.

"That's right, it's Nelly." I gulp. "He's with Nelly." My voice grows soft, wondering it if was all coincidence, or a sign. Either way, it struck my grief in a way I cannot fathom.

Unable to hold it all in, I fell on my knees and wept like a child. Mika waits for me to resurface and when I do, she is right there in my field of vision. She wipes the tears off of my cheek and hooks her pinkie onto mine.

She smiles with storms in her eyes, matching mine. We were lightning and thunder. When we pull apart, we create a storm. No amount of bombs or guns was going to trifle with our winds.

In that moment as we pulled away, I made a strong realization that would power me through the remainder of our journey; This little girl needed me as much as I needed her.

Snapping our fingers, I let the words fall out of my mouth.

"I pinkie promise we won't die."

That is a promise I'll make sure not to break twice.

We've learned a lot in the past few days living in the forest. Mika and I eventually grew tired of eating fish and pursued other alternatives. We ate a handful of eggs we could find from nests up in the trees and a few retrievable woodland critters. At first, I had to slaughter them out of Mika's sight as it made her squeamish. She hated it when they didn't die after I shot them because that meant I had to break their necks open.

"It's the humane way," I tell her. "Killing them quickly will stop them from feeling pain longer than they need to be. Sometimes suffering is a consequence worse than death."

"No." she signs tapping her fingers like a crab.

"Yes," I reply as I set our dinner over the fire. We both gazed at it, thinking of Maxine. We hadn't spoken of him since the attack.

"Think all you want, but we both know I'm right."

Two days later she wanted to practice catching our meals on her own. She asked for my help when it came to snapping their necks, but the rest was on her. She had no issue skinning or catching the others. From there, we created a system of equally divided tasks and a set of rules for each other.

The fundamental rule is to follow the river regardless of what happens to either one of us. We needed to survive as though Maxine's soul was lingering with ours. It was the key motivator for us to survive together. The rest of the rules had to do with safety. An example is gun safety. It reminded me of the days when Max and I were taken to a kiddie shooting range. I'd place small targets and Maxine would shoot at them with a toy gun. We'd take turns and slowly learn how to use the real ones when our parents thought we were ready.

Like they back then, I informed Mika of all the do's and don'ts of using a gun. I waited till we felt far enough from any soldiers to shoot some practice rounds. They caught up to us a few times but never managed to catch us fully. The forest felt like our greatest friend. Mika hid well as her green jumpsuit was like camouflage and I grew accustomed to the patterns of the hills and trees. The closest thing that had ever reached us was their bullets. They ran after us and shot with no regard for our lives. We hid in ditches and played pretend with the blood that stained our clothes.

One soldier made the mistake of turning their back on me and ended up with a slashed throat. It was the quietest and most efficient method for me to get away without having the officer draw attention to us. I snatched their weapon and made a run for it with Mika. We were relieved to see that none of us got injured. I gave her a scare a few times when she saw my trousers stained in blood while we were washing our clothes further down the river path we found. I explained to her it was a normal phenomenon and nothing to worry about. **She didn't** believe me at first, but after a few days had gone by and there was less of it, she was less concerned.

We slowly got used to our new lives and met other kids like us along the way. They were the few remaining survivors whom the G.C.P.O.A. officers captured. We found them in a similar situation to what Mika and I were in. They were caught one by one and lured into a difficult spot in the forest. They were bound in chains and gagged. On their ankle was the tracker band beeping in an earsplitting noise.

Mika lures the officer away from them and falls for our trap. The officer squirms in my choke hold and fails in their endeavors to shoot Mika. I break their neck instantaneously seeing as they were far from human. If they're going to behave like murderers, I will treat them as such. Mika grew used to this new demeanor of mine, despite not entirely agreeing with my choices. There was a small portion of innocence within her that didn't want me to kill these soldiers, but when they pointed their guns, she knew they gave us no choice but for me to act as such.

She silently prayed over the officer and left me with the task of releasing our fellow survivors. They were a pair of fraternal twins, one boy, and one girl. They both wore light pink outfits. Possibly the last pinks left. I recognize them from my math class. They held still when they recognized me. I ripped off their trackers without electrocuting either one of us and broke their restraints. They stare at me in awe, unable to wrap their hand around my superhuman-like abilities. Yet, my strength was far from the weird part. There wasn't any logical explanation for what happened next.

A sparking sensation of pins and needles course through my hands from when I broke their trackers.

"Why are your eyes glowing like that?" the girl shouts, alarmed.

"Huh?"

Sparking the tips of my fingers are bolts of electricity. I flick my wrists, trying to fan it off, but that only results in a power surge within me and a static shock, striking a nearby tree. It goes up into flames and alerts the other officers. Mika and the twins stared at me with utter shock.

We hear the voices of officers alerting the others to the tree and make a run for it. They were too distracted by the fire to deal with us. Based on what I've witnessed these last few days, large tanks and a few government automobiles were used to spray the tree down before the fire could catch any further. It's how the forest didn't get burned down when the bombings and explosions occurred during the escape.

Alongside the twins, together we formed a pack and sprinted past the G.C.P.O.A. until we had nothing but the moon to be our guide. We sat by the river and ate a few of the rabbits I shot on the way there. They cooked perfectly fine with the fire Mika had set. I skinned them and used their fur to keep Mika's hands warm. She wasn't too fond of it.

Mika and I shared a rabbit and gave the twins each of their own. They didn't say much and went at it. Within seconds, all that was left were bits of chewed bones. Like a silent agreement, we didn't talk about what happened. They didn't seem to be in the mood, and neither was I. All

I could think about was when I tried to rub the green serum over Max's wound when I tried to save him. I was always used to injecting it, but never once thought about the potential ability it could give me if I were to coax it on my skin like lotion.

It's no wonder why I felt like my hands were vibrating rather than shaking. I thought it had been from the sudden shock after what had happened to Max or the chills from when I went back into the cold water to catch Mika and me food. Now that I think about it, I don't remember the serum washing away like the blood and dirt did. The green seeped into my skin and vanished by the time I finished digging Maxine's grave. Minutes after it was over, and I entered the plunge pool, that's when the sensation began.

I didn't want to raise any suspicions with Billy and Tracy, the twins, so I waited until they fell asleep to test out my newest ability. Mika unsuspectingly followed my tail and saw me trying to spark my hands in the middle of the forest. She taps my shoulder and crosses her arms into an X.

I yank out the gun in my pocket and point the muzzle at her. I recognized the shape of her silhouette and lowered my weapon. "Gosh, Mika! I almost shot you!"

I tuck the weapon back into my right pocket and try to shoo her away.

"Go back to sleep. This is dangerous."

She shakes her head and plants herself in front of me.

"Real mature. Look, I don't want to hurt you with whatever is going on, so I need you to leave."

She waves at me to continue and signs "I am not going anywhere."

"Ugh! Fine! But stay back a little."

She obeys and walks back a fair distance away from me. I wave my hands in the air a few times and no reaction happens. I tried a few other poses and movements to see if anything was willing to come out. Nothing.

Mika grasps a pile of dirt and throws it directly at me.

"Mika!" I exclaim. "Ugh, that didn't work!"

I dust myself over and over to get rid of the specks of dirt caught on Xander's purple jumpsuit. The vibrating starts and at the final stroke of dusting, sparks fly out from the tips of my fingers.

Mika's mouth gaped open in excitement.

I run my hands against the fabric, and the sparks continue. "Static electricity! The serum must've acted as a super-conductor on a superficial spectrum, causing me to conduct electricity the way I do!"

Mika raises her eyebrows, spelling out "In English, please."

"Remember the green stuff that I rubbed on Max?" Her expression darkens at the mention of his name. She slowly bobs her head up and down, and I continue.

"The stuff acted as a binding agent whenever we got hurt. Whatever they put in it made me super strong. Because it was in my hands for so long, it must've also acted as a conductor of electricity. In other words, I have super strength AND electrical powers."

Mika and I jump in excitement at my newfound ability. Like most happy things, it quickly turned into terror.

What if the facility finds out about the serum and makes the officers into super soldiers?

What if they get us and I can't fight them this time?

Wait.

Oh, no.

What if they use it on the kids still in the facility?

I can see it now. They use kids to lure the others, and in return, they meet their end. If and when we get to HQ, I will need to spill them the details in hopes they can handle it. The problem is, when on earth will we get there?

Setting aside my worries for the morning, Mika and I return to the space we left the twins. They remained asleep, practically dying of exhaustion. I could only assume they had gone through the worst during their time inside of the forest. They were weak and frail compared to Mika and me. It's propounding how they were able to last as long as they did. They didn't have the supplies we had or anything with them to protect themselves other than each other. Their closeness reminded me a lot of how Max and I ~~use to~~ are.

I tried everything in me not to think or speak about him in the past tense, especially regarding our closeness. I kept his baseball constantly in the pocket of my jumpsuit as a reminder of that. I ran my hands through it whenever I felt I needed some aspect of his presence (mostly during the nights).

It soothed me enough to calm me down, but never to keep my eyes closed. I was scared of falling asleep, for if I did, I might dream of him like I did with Xander. I wasn't ready to have such an encounter. At least not when my judgment is clouded with ravaging beasts of vengeance and barbaric manslaughter.

No.

It must be under different circumstances.

Not to worry, I have but one remedy.

To prevent the titans from tainting the rest of me, I've kept the memories and pieces of my joy locked inside my internal cave, next to my heart, with Midnight and River, where they are protected.

Someday they'll see the light, and by then, I'll be ready.

30

It's been a week since the escape, and we still have yet to reach HQ. I was starting to second-guess myself. What if I'm going in the wrong direction? What if there are no headquarters? It also didn't make sense how we hadn't arrived there by now. The trip was supposed to be three days in total. There must be something we're doing wrong.

Something *I'm* doing wrong.

It felt like the blame was on no one but me. To them, I was like some sort of survival expert. The older twins looked up to me, and obviously, so did Mika. They relied on me for everything.

"El, how do you do this?"

"El, does this look fully cooked?"

"El, where do we go to do number two?"

It tediously became overbearing as everyone was at their limits, including me. I had to throw myself into the river a few times this morning because I was close to zapping one of the twins, Billy. I was surprised how the boy made it this far with his twin.

To stay somewhat mellow during our travels to the next destination, I kept my hands at my sides and hummed a melody of the Steven the Dog theme song. Mika sensed my apprehension and handed me a flower for me to smell along the way. I took it and tucked it in my ear. I would've put it in my hair, but…it's not there. Max would've probably laughed at my attempt. He's pretty good at laughing when he isn't supposed to. It's another reason why he ~~used to~~ get in trouble in school often.

"I'm tired." moaned Billy as he scraped his heels to the ground.

"We all are! Stop your complaining." Tracy elbows him. "Look, you're bothering Mika."

"No, I'm not!"

"Yes, you are! Stop yelling! She doesn't like when we yell."

"What do you know? She barely talks!"

"If you tried to communicate with her, maybe you'd know better!"

Mika covers her ears and walks closer to me.

"Oh, look what you've done!"

"What I've done? You're yelling too! Besides, who cares what she thinks!"

"I do! I care about what she thinks!"

For a pair of older teenagers, they sure lacked the maturity Mika and I had. They were always arguing and obnoxiously at each other's throats. Billy frequently complained, and Tracy would try to calm him down; it never worked.

"How long do we need to continue like this, Tracy? For all we know, we're getting nowhere!"

"It's better than being dead!"

"I would rather be dead! At least I wouldn't have to deal with you! You're always bossing me and everywhere you pointed us to go, got us in trouble! That officer should've shot me instead of being saved by two little kids!"

Tracy's eyes go vacant, lost in memory. She clutches a small shred of paper in the palm of her right hand tightly and bites her lower lip, weighing her words. Since we took them in, she always seems to be the one holding back her remarks; just the way I did with Maxine. Except their relationship was different. He's been crossing the line, and it's been affecting her. I've caught Tracy crying a couple of times while Billy tended to his tasks, completely fine.

"Is it?" I intervene.

"Is it what?" He jeers, stomping his foot.

"Is it better than being dead?"

"At this rate."

"Is that so?" I yield my weapon to the side of his head.

"Oh god!" he squeals, like a chipmunk.

"I can make your wish come true. Say the word and I'll shoot."

He freezes up and keeps his mouth tightly shut.

"Please don't kill him. He's all I have," his twin sister begs, crawling on her knees.

I ignore her and press the weapon deeper into his skull.

"Well?" I ask Billy, weighing the gun in my hands.

"Billy, please don't let her shoot you. I need you, Billy. We already lost Ma and Pa."

"I'm waiting." I taunt, speaking over his sister's cries.

"You're bluffing."

"After seeing me kill several soldiers, you really think another body is going to affect me?" I take his wrist and pin his arm to his back.

"Agh." he yelps.

"I'm going to ask you a question and you better answer this time," I whisper into his ear.

"Billy!"

"Is surviving with your sister worse than death?"

"N-n-n-o."

"I can't hear you."

"N-n-o! It's not worse than death! I'm sorry! I am so sorry Tracy!" He stutters, giving his sister an apologetic gaze. "I didn't mean it."

"Good." I move the weapon away from his head and motion him to comfort his sister. I stop him mid-step, whispering into his ear. "I lost my brother. Don't let her lose hers."

I release his shoulder and continue to follow the stream, keeping my finger over the trigger. As Billy apologizes to Tracy, Mika skips next to me with a stick in her hand.

She was never fond of direct physical contact, so she made up a medium she was comfortable with. She would hold one end of her stick and I would hold the other. The only times I'd held her hand or carried her were when she told me she wanted me to. It made her incredibly happy whenever I complied with her needs.

"Did I scare you back there?" I ask.

She shakes her head and makes the sign for "lie".
The corner of my upper lip tugs upward into a
mischievous grin.

"I hope you know you are a very bright girl,
Mika."

She giggles and follows beside me.

# 31

"Tray, you know what's weird," Billy comments as he comes back with another pair of dead rabbits I sent for him to catch. He was getting good at it in comparison to the other tasks I had him complete. Trust me when I say there was a reason why he wasn't allowed to start a fire anymore. He wasn't good with laundry either as most of our clothes ended up being lost in the river no thanks to him.

"What?"

I take the rabbits from him and rinse them out with the water I stored in my water bottle. When they felt clean enough, I skinned away their fur using a pocketknife I stole from a companion I had killed a few days ago. They had their initials engraved on the side of the blade spelling G.D.Q. Tracy suggested I get rid of the knife as she didn't want us to have "bad juju" from it. Contrary to her advice, I kept the knife and used it as my own.

With clean cuts, I run the blade various times over the rabbit until I reach the meat. It reminded me of how my mother prepared the raccoon meal. When she realized

I knew what it was, she allowed me back into the kitchen and I helped her prepare it for dinner.

"We haven't encountered that many companions since El and Mika found us," he says, stretching his arms to the sky.

"Huh, now that you've mentioned it, it has been awfully peaceful these last few days," Her brows raise as her chin tilts in my direction.

I stopped midway from skinning the second rabbit when it registered that they were talking to me.

"El."

"Huh?" I blink, turning to her.

"Billy has mentioned that he found it weird that the companions haven't been coming after us since we paired off with you guys. Isn't that strange? When we escaped, we encountered those punks every single day. Now, it's like we run into one or two of those guys every other day."

I stop skinning the rabbit.

"What?"

"Billy said-"

"I know what he said." I cut her off and set the rabbit down on a flat rock. I press the palm to my head, steadying myself. "Oh, my gosh."

"El what's wrong?"

"This is bad. Really really bad." I stab the pocketknife into a tree.

"El!"

"Something bad is going to happen."

"Like what?"

"I don't know." I press my hands at the sides of my brain, fighting to ease my headache.

"Then why do you think something bad is going to happen?"

"Because they do! Right when we think things are calm and happy, the G.C.P.O.A. always comes in and ruins it! They're planning something. Something real bad. They always do! They're like those sore losers who always have to have the last laugh!"

Billy chuckles at the sore loser part, and Tracy glares at him.

"El, calm down. You're going to give yourself a heart attack." Tracy circles me and tries to sit me down.

"I think I'm having one right now."

"El, it's going to be okay. Whatever happens, happens. We'll face whatever they throw at us together." Billy reasons.

"Yes! Exactly like Billy says. We've managed to get this far. Whatever they're planning won't hinder us any more than whatever they've been doing. We'll face it together, you, me, Billy, and Mika."

"Mika." I gasp. "Where's Mika?"

"She's in the stream," Tracy states.

"MIKA!" I roar hysterically.

"El, it's okay."

"MIKA!"

"Look, look, there she is." Billy points in the direction of the stream. Mika trots to us, holding a handful of berries she has found. They stained her fingers with hues of blue, purple, and red.

"Oh, thank god." I sigh. I bend over to my knees, dangling my head upside down to see in between my legs.

"El, are you okay?" Tracy puts her hand on my shoulder. "If you need to talk about something, I'm right here for you. If this is about losing your brother-"

"It's not." I lie. The hairs on my arms go up and the tingling makes its way through me. Tracy removes her hold and scoots a fair distance from me. "Agh! Why now?"

"Because you're anxious. Look, panicking and stressing yourself out isn't going to fix anything. We've been at it for days. I think it's time to give ourselves a break while we can."

"Or, we should use this time to keep moving!"

"El, it's getting close to sundown. It's dangerous! Billy and I tried that once and almost got killed by a coyote."

"It was a wolf." Billy corrects her.

"Not helping Billy!"

"I can handle a wolf." I punched a tree, leaving a chipped dent. The crows fly out of their nest and make their annoying caws. "It will be more dangerous when they completely wipe us out!"

"They wouldn't," Billy says.

"Exactly." Tracy nods.

"Because if they wanted to do that, they would've done that already. Ouch! Tracy, that hurts!" He rubs the side of his arm.

"Not. Helping." She bares her teeth at him. Speaking with her eyes, she signals for him to play with Mika. I quickly strengthen myself out of my hunchback and grab my backpack.

"El, please don't tell me you're packing." She rips it from my hands and dangles it over my head. Our height difference was pretty significant, considering she was one of the older pinks.

"Hey! Give it back!"

"Not until I knock some sense into you. I mean, look at us! We are not in the right spot to be traveling, especially during this time. You haven't even made our dinner yet! Imagine how hungry Mika will be."

I stop reaching for the backpack at the mention of Mika. Not once on this trip had I ever made Mika go hungry. Like how my parents were with Maxine and me, I made sure we'd always have something in our stomachs. "La comida te dará vida." my mother would say.

"We'll leave in the morning when we get a nice long night of rest," Tracy says softly.

She gestures to me to sit down on a log, and I bitterly comply. She tosses the backpack at my feet, and I let it sit there. Inside were my ugly tennis shoes bulging at the seams of the zipper. They didn't compare to the combat boots I stole off of an officer's dead body. The boots were made of fine waterproof material and had a small pocket to store my pocketknife in. I kept my old pair of shoes in case I needed to briskly slip on a pair of shoes. Unlike the boots, the tennis shoes didn't require effort to put them on.

Staring at them, I noticed how terrible condition my shoes were in. The soles hardly had any cushion from all the traveling we'd been through and had irremovable stains that haunted my memories. Mika's shoes were far worse than mine, considering she didn't have a pair of stolen shoes like I did. Blisters covered her swollen feet like no other. Her favorite remedy was chilling her feet in the river water until it was time to put them back on again.

Maybe Tracy was right.

I lift my head as I hear Mika squealing. A smile plants on my face and I wave back at her. After the argument Billy had with Tracy, those two had gotten awfully close. She let Billy carry her on his shoulders and control him like a puppet. She'd run her hands in his hair and tugged on his curls based on the direction she wanted him to go. He'd happily oblige and run around gleefully.

Tracy notices the change in my expression and sits closer to me. I kick the backpack to the side and tilt my head to the clouds. I've caught myself imagining Maxine in them a few times. While I think it's highly unlikely, his spirit haunted me. I saw him in bits of my reflection in the water and heard his voice in the wind like whispers. At night, I avoided him altogether. I'd hold his ball and rub my thumb over its texture to stop myself from seeing him bleeding. I hated myself for remembering him at his worst.

I take a deep breath and snap myself out of it. "You're right," I admitted to Tracy.

"I knew you'd come around." She smiles.

"No, uh. Well, yes. What I mean is, you were right about what you said earlier." I sigh. "About Maxine…"

"Ele-"

"Please don't say my name. The last two people who said it died." I warn her. The tingling stayed persistent on my fingertips. They reminded me of electric eels.

We both keep our eyes on Billy and Mika, watching them giggle and laugh.

"I'm not going to die, *Elen-*"

"Stop!" I hover my palm over her lips. "Please."

The corners of her mouth deepen into a sympathetic frown. I withdraw my electric eels, shaking my head.

"Elena," she says finally.

"Why?" I cry.

"Because your name is not a curse, it's a cure. Those people said your name because they care about you. Look, I'm still here, aren't I?" She lifts from her seat and twists in her heels, dancing with her arms in the air. She reaches out for me, and I gawk, baffled.

"I'm not going to die because I said your name." she asserts, sitting back down next to me. I don't meet her brown spheres. I keep my focus on Mika and Billy.

Mika got off his shoulders and gave Billy a water break. They resumed their games by bouncing around in a hopscotch they drew on a patch of mud.

"How can you be so sure? What if we never make it to the headquarters? Then what?"

The corners of her mouth deepen into a sympathetic frown.

"I promise you we'll manage. As long as we got each other," she says softly.

"Promise is a big word." I retaliate.

"And I intend to meet it. You saw what happened to the pinks. They wiped us out like nothing, yet Billy and I survived regardless. We've lost several people that day," she says, getting teary-eyed. She pulls out a small piece of paper, admiring it longingly. "Including my boyfriend."

"You had a boyfriend?" I break out of my gaze and turn to her. She remained tilted downward to the paper.

"Yeah," she smiles fondly. "I have known him since we were little. He was Billy's best friend. Billy wasn't so happy when he found out about us, but soon enough, he came around. We were going to go to junior prom together, Drew and I."

Her eyelids droop longingly. She reminisced as she illustrated the dress she was going to wear and the future they had planned after graduating from high school. They were going to attend the same local college that was located in their small town called Flatio.

"We were so close to having the time of our lives," Her shoulders sag closer to her chest. "But then..."

"But then the G.C.P.O.A. came," I murmur.

She shakes her head up and down, tears falling like the rain.

"It's normal to feel this way. I hope you know that. You and I, our pain, are the same. We both lost somebody we loved. Billy still refuses to think about our Ma and Pa, but for his sake, I do." She tucks the note in her pocket and resumes her focus back on Billy. "We're all scared. Hell, you saw how scared I was when I thought you'd shoot Billy."

For some reason, that made me chuckle.

"Anyhow, my point is, we all had come this far despite the odds thrown against us. Whether or not the headquarters exists, we still have each other. If we have to, we'll leave the forest and seek refuge elsewhere."

"Is our food ready yet?" Billy whines, rubbing his stomach. Mika mimics him, pouting.

Tracy and I laugh and resume our tasks. I rip the knife out of the tree and pick up the second rabbit I was skinning. Mika sparks a flame with the flint and steel I let her keep. Billy gathers sticks he found and feeds the tiger, keeping it tame until I finish skinning the last rabbit. With time, the tingling sensation steadily disperses, and I return to my normal state.

As we wait for our food to cook, Tracy dances with the tiger, controlling the shadows around her with the steps of a ballerina. Mika and Billy join her, clapping and chanting silly songs. I joined them in a particular one.

We are the pinks.
Mighty and free.

Tracy says the next line, pointing a stick to the sky like a sword.

We are the pinks.

As brave as we could be.

Billy disperses a few he finds, and together, we wave them for the remainder of the chant.

Our color should not matter,
And our people were shattered.

Tracy points at me to say a line. I think on my feet and let the words spill out of my mouth.

We are far from broken
and truth must be spoken,

You have ruined our trust,
And this system is unjust.

We will shout and scream,
As we are human as we can be.

We link together in a circle and bounce around the tiger. It roars with our voices.

Tonight, we unite,

until we are free.

Screaming with a final triumph, the tiger rises and springs our shadows to life.

We are the pinks!

We dine on the rabbits, sharing our life stories like we do every night. I help Mika chop up her favorite parts and eat the rest. Nearing the end of our night Tracy pulls me aside and whispers a few words of encouragement to my ears.

"El, you're the bravest and smartest person I know, never forget to show it." she pats the top of my head gently and situates herself next to her twin. Mika and I let them bond as we count the constellations we find.

It was a good day to be alive.

We spotted the G.C.P.O.A.'s newest tool flying over the trees. They were miniature drones armed with small bullets. The drones were terrifying at first, but once we shot them down, they became bearable. The tiny machines were equally annoying as a large fly buzzing in your bedroom. After a point in time, you get used to the fly and kill it out of spite. It's incredibly satisfying.

The beauty of it all was how the drones worked to our advantage. One companion couldn't see me walk past her because she was preoccupied with controlling those pesky drones to see me coming.

It made them easier to take out.

I'd sneak up on them from behind and attack them on-site. Plenty have died at my hands because they attempted to harm my friends. Like Mika, Billy and Tracy weren't keen on the idea of taking the companions' lives unless they were given no other choice. They left me to do the dirty work and took on other roles. For their sake, I let them, as it was less of an emotional toll.

Tracy's first kill kept her awake for an entire night as she kept tossing and turning. She cried and cried in

Billy's arms, telling him how a horrible human being she was.

I decided from there that I would take care of the companions. As a team, they were mainly comfortable stealing the dead companion's supplies, as they wanted to stock up on weapons and gear. It didn't help to see what I did to the body, but it was a simple enough task for Tracy, Billy, and Mika to stomach.

As for the drones, they were perfect practice for Mika's target training. She shot those buggers down with a small pistol I gave her. I snatched it during my hunt for dinner. It was at the hip of a companion who erroneously tried to ambush me underneath some bushes. It wasn't big like mine and had a smaller number of bullets.

It was the most 'child-friendly' one we had.

Seeing how well we took control of their drones; I grew to believe our chances to make it out of the forest alive to be true. We were slowly making progress and scrambling for better options during our endeavors.

Our biggest mission yet was hijacking the tanks.

"It will get us to our destination faster," Billy suggests.

We all thought he was mad for such an idea, but the further we followed the ways of the water, it became increasingly evident we needed a mode of transportation to get through the remainder of the journey.

Wait.

Transportation.

A small idea crosses my mind.

What if maybe, *just maybe*, we got the three-day journey all wrong? What if it was a three-day journey, but with an assumption we traveled on a vehicle of some sort? If that is the case, there is still hope of finding the headquarters (or making it out of the forest, whatever comes first).

"I don't know about this. I think it's safer for us to keep going the way we are." Tracy replies apprehensively.

"Come on Tray, what's an adventure without taking any risks?" Billy asserts.

I do admit, Billy had a point. A ride inside a tank sounds more fun than butchering the soles of our shoes for another hundred miles. We could make it out of the forest in no time.

I stare at the clouds as we walk, dazed, and distracted by the idea of making it out of here. I thought about all the things I would tell my parents when I reunited with them. The escape. The tests. The deaths. The people I have killed to get to them. Everything.

Well, everything except for Maxine. I still couldn't control myself whenever I tried to explain to the twins what had happened. Electricity would spout out of me like some sort of discombobulated toaster. Mika had to stop me from continuing to make sure I didn't electrocute anyone. I had to excuse myself from them to deep breaths and wait for the sensation to fade.

That same day at night, I made sure everyone, including Mika, had been asleep. I snuck away from them and talked to the closest Nelly I could find. I'd let myself melt in front of her, clutching Maxine's baseball without burning or breaking it. Nelly would stare at me, protecting her nest from the foot of a berry bush. I felt awful when my power surge got the best of me and electrocuted Nelly. I held her all night until the morning scared me away, like the monster that I am.

I still hadn't recovered from the incident. It disturbed me relentlessly. Insomnia trickled through my bloodstream, causing my exhaustion to rule the entirety of my body. Strangely, I owned it. It felt like a reciprocal punishment for letting Max go the way he did.

I deserve to be miserable.

"What do you think, El? You've gotten us this far. I trust you. It's your call." Tracy turns to me, swatting away a mosquito hovering over the bridge of her curved nose.

I shift my hand away from the pocket of the baseball and snap my attention to them. I still found the dynamic to be odd seeing how they asked me for guidance despite being older than me.

"Hmmm." I move my mouth to the side indecisively.

Clasping his hands together, Billy whispered a silent prayer in hopes of picking his side for once. We take a break by the stream and refill our water bottles. While I think, Mika crouches at my feet, messaging her swollen ankles.

Her feet have gotten worse. She had bigger bunions than me, and constantly needed to take off her shoes for some relief. I gave her mine because her green ones didn't fit her anymore. There were too many bugs and critters on the ground for me to let her stay barefoot.

I felt guilty for not being able to provide more for her.

"I think we should make at least one attempt. If it goes south, we'll go back to walking. We'll need to be extra careful." I scan their faces for approval.

Billy punches the air with glee and splashes some water at Mika playfully. She returns the gesture by splashing the water from her water bottle on him. I catch some of the spillage and scold them both. Billy apologizes on their behalf and stops altogether.

"Billy, if you want to get a tank, you need to focus."

"Okay, okay. My bad."

"Good. In terms of the tanks, we'll need to consider a strong and secure plan. These tanks are always filled with officers. We need to figure out a way to lure them out long enough for all of us to get in and drive out of there."

"And how do we do that?" Tracy asks.

"I know. I know." Billy raises his hand like a schoolboy, jumping excitedly. I had to tell him to stop as I progressively felt dizzy seeing him bounce. He obediently halts in place and strategically proposes his idea. At his side, he hauls his small revolver out of the pocket of his clothes and shoots at a tree next to Tracy.

Perhaps it was a bad idea for him to have a weapon. Granted, we were all armed. It was better than being defenseless. They all trained under me and have yet to injure themselves.

She squeals and hits his shoulder when he tucks the revolver back to its secured place. He then confidently brushes his dark hair out of his face, flexing his arms and legs. "With this bad boy, I'll shoot at the sides of the tank and have them chase me while you guys run inside the tank."

"And if they don't?" Tracy crosses her arms.

"Don't what? Chase me?"

"Yes. What if they shoot you instead? Then what?"

"They won't. I mean, who wouldn't want to chase after this face? Don't forget, I was the best quarterback at Deerwell High. I'm extremely irresistible."

Mika rolls her eyes and Tracy scoffs.

"You're an idiot."

"You doubt me too much. If they shoot, I'll run. After all, we all know I'm the fastest here," he says pridefully. "They'll never catch me."

"Oh please! You're going to get yourself and us killed!"

"Oh, lighten up Tray. It's a good plan."

"No! That's a stupid plan! Right El? El?"

I trip over my boots, falling halfway into the river. Tracy managed to catch my arm in time to keep the other half of me afloat. Luckily, none of my supplies got wet.

I grip her arm and let her reel me out of the shallow end. I shake off the excess water, holding back the reeling pain in the back of my head.

"Shoot." I curse, blinking out of my haze.

"Are you alright? You look like you need some rest."

"Yeah, I'm feeling dehydrated, that's all." I fight my fatigue and force myself to focus.

"If you need to take a break, we can set up-"

"No, no more breaks! We already did that thirty minutes ago. I'll refill my water bottle and we'll continue to follow the river. I'll rest when we hit sundown."

"Are you sure?" Billy asks, concerned.

"Yes, I'm sure. As for the plan, as stupid as it is, I don't see any other option. One of us will need to distract the companions. I was saving this for an emergency, but this seems to call for it."

I open my backpack and pull out my latest stolen item. It reminded me of a miniature bowling ball as it was dense and weighty despite being small. The bomb glowed purple and had a small button on its side. Based on the weapons I've seen before, this invention was the latest technology they had yet. All I had to do was hold the bomb's silver button for three seconds and toss it in the direction I wanted it to explode. It resembled the one that they threw at us back in the waterfall incident, except there was no need to pull out the pin.

Maybe this time, I'll be able to return their lovely gesture. End their lives like how they ended Maxine's. You can argue it was a bullet that ended him, but bullets and bombs were all the same to me at this rate.

I hold the bomb in the center for them to examine its glorious composition.

"Woah," Billy gasps, alarmed.

Tracy covers her hand over her mouth with wide eyes. "El, you didn't." She gently touches the surface of the bomb with her index finger, careful to stray away from the silver button.

"One of us will need to lure them with this. To make things easier, I'll be the one to do it."

Mika frowns and shakes her head in disapproval, swaying the pigtails Tracy had braided on the opposite sides of her head. The woven blond locks reminded me of the rope I had used to choke out a companion not too long ago.

"Look, as far as I can tell, I'm the only one here who has been able to take out these officers without feeling awful the next day. It'll save yourselves the heartache."

"El, you feel just as awful as we do."

"No, I don't."

"You're confused."

"I'm not confused, I'm angry," I growled, tucking away the bomb into my pocket. "If anyone should do this, it's me."

Tracy's apprehension branched over to Mika and Billy. His glee fell to anxiousness, following Mika's relentless lip-biting. They notice my hands tremble and put some distance away from me. Tracy had to peel away Mika to stop her from getting any closer.

"Maybe we should-"

"No, I want to carry on with this plan," I assert, cutting Billy off. "I want to do this."

"El,"

"Please," I pleaded.

"It won't bring him back."

"I know it won't. Nothing will, which is why I have to do this." I breathe those words out of my lungs as though someone had trapped them in my chest. They exchange unnerving glances as I fight the sparks flickering on the surface of my thumbprints.

It's one thing to read a person's facial expression, but when your ability makes your emotions visible, as they did like mine, it makes you feel incredibly vulnerable. I despised how I hadn't mastered a method to tame it. It made me seem more unstable than I am.

"We'll think about it. How about we stock up on supplies and discuss this at night? Maybe we can come up with a similar plan. Something less risky." Tracy takes a sip out of her water bottle and gestures for us to continue walking.

Mika groans, hunching over to Billy, who is willing enough to carry Mika for the rest of our journey. I comply for the sake of peace and follow behind them with an ache persisting at the sides of my head.

33

None of us were prepared for what awaited in the dark. We were blindsided and oblivious to their foul low blow tactics, thinking we were going to have another restful slumber. It started off calmly until they struck us like demons of the night. They used the time to sharpen their talons and thrived in the shadows, lurking until our fire of hope couldn't burn any longer. To this day, I blame myself for not staying awake. Had I allowed my insomnia to linger further, maybe I would've seen them coming.

It was all wishful thinking now.

After our long journey, when nightfall had hit, we sat together, formulating the best plan possible to take on the tank for the next day. We decided it was best for us to gather as many weapons as possible so that if any of us were attacked, we'd be prepared. As for my personal endeavors, I remain resilient in my perils to be the human sacrifice. They tried to talk me out of it, but I was firm in my decision.

I had it all mentally planned.

Like a peacock, I'd strut in all my glory, waving my arms and legs like feathers, captivating their bloodthirsty, heinous attention to me. They'd mindlessly follow me into the forest like a pack of hungry hyenas, grinning on both sides as if they had me. But they don't.

I'd intently lure them into my Roman arena of death, where the trees became the bars of a cage and the audience were the creatures of the forest. Shifting to my true form, my feathers would turn into fur. I'd be the hungry lion and they would turn into helpless gladiators. I'd release my roars of anguish left from my grief and allow the electricity to pour out of my hands and sink into their skin like canines. They'll fall below my knees, heaving breathlessly with mercy. Though, I wouldn't kill them.

Not yet.

I'd make sure they stay alive. Alive to witness their bodies burn as I climb a tree like Max, and I ~~used to~~ do. In honor of him, I'd release the hold of my thumb from the cold metal button and throw it at them like a baseball. The banshees would sing, stealing their souls in a wondrous, vengeful symphony.

"I think I'm going to catch some sleep." Tracy yawns. She removes her vest where she kept her weapons and tosses it aside. "All this thinking is making my head hurt."

Billy agrees and piles his leaves for them to rest their backs on. They were hardly visible as the fire was slowly shrinking. I wanted to do one last thing, so I pulled Mika aside. She thought I was going to show her a trick relating to my ability and frowned when I didn't.

"Not tonight. I have something else in mind." I hush. Removing the object from my pocket, I carefully held it and told her to close her eyes. She obeys and I tuck it into her tiny palms. Upon contact as her fingers touch the ridges, she immediately recognizes it, getting teary-eyed. She shoves the ball back to me and tightens her hand over mine.

"Mika, I want you to hold on to it."

She shakes her shoulders and applies pressure.

"You can give it back to me when it's over. I want you to keep it safe in the meantime."

"No."

"Mika."

"No."

"Liste-"

"No!"

"Stop!" I yell at her. She shrinks back, keeping her hands intertwined with mine, enclosing the ball. "Sorry."

I sigh and loosen my hold. "I know this seems scary. I can see it." I open her hand and unravel the ball out in the open. "You're scared that I'm giving you the ball because you think I might die. Am I right?"

She slowly nods her head, shifting the braids at the sides of her ears.

"Well, I'm not." I toss the ball in the air and catch it with my other hand. "I'm giving this to you as a sign that I will make it out alive."

She raises her eyebrow solemnly.

"I want that ball back. We both know this. But I don't want it until we finish this mission. Think of it as a way for you to hold me accountable." I hold up the ball, balancing it on my palm. "My reward for making it out alive is this ball."

She taps her foot and crosses her arms skeptically.

"What will it take for you to hold this ball for me?"

The light bulb turns on over her little blond head. She holds up her pinkie to me, holding it up stiffly.

"Really? I thought we already made that promise."

She holds her pinkie higher, inching it closer to my face.

She's a stubborn one. Like Maxine.

As of late, I see glimpses of him in her. It made me sentimental and miss him more than ever, which I didn't think could be possible. In some sort of cruel way, it made me think about what it would be like if they had switched places. Would've I saw bits of her in him? How would our trip change? Was there ever a way I could've protected them both and sacrificed myself instead?

"Fine," I mumble, hooking my finger over hers. "I pinkie promise we don't die." I toss the ball in the air, and she catches it. She skips beside me and together we return to Tracy and Billy fighting over a blanket they shared.

Mika giggles and I lay on the floor in my designated spot. I always liked the spot where I could lay my back to a tree with a thick trunk. It felt safer. Like someone was keeping me from slipping away. As my head bent back and my spine aligned to a comfortable position, all of my senses were lost. The sandman poured too much on me.

If I had just stayed awake.

I didn't know how long it was. At the moment, when mayhem woke my slumber, there wasn't enough time for me to process anything. The fire had gone out and the voices of my fellow friends hummed against my partially damaged ears. Tracy's shriek was the most prominent for me to hear. She had a certain pitch that was as sharp as broken glass. I sadly only heard it a few times as I grappled with reality.

"Get your hands off me!" she shouted. Crunches of leaves shifted underneath her makeshift bed. "Billy! Someone! Help me!"

I abruptly lifted myself away from the tree and felt a hand grip against my ankle. It tugged on me like a shark, making little to no noise in comparison to the grunting officer strangling Tracy.

"Tracy!" I yell. The hold on my leg twisted furiously as though they were about to snap my leg in half.

"El! Help!" She wheezes as the officer pins her.

"I'm coming." I shift my leg upward attempting to slip out of the grasp on my foot. In the process, I fell right into the center of the fire pit. The soot of the fire sizzles my arms, wriggling inside of me. All the scars that I thought had finally healed reopened.

"Augh!" I yelp.

I bite the side of my mouth and dig my elbows deeper into the pile to scooch closer to her. Much to my luck, I caught a bit of the debris in my eyes, adding further to the darkness, (as if it wasn't already dark enough). I blinked several times to find her silhouette and kicked at the hand ferociously. I reached to the side, trying to feel Mika's body in hopes that she had a chance to get away.

Nothing.

"Billy!"

"Mika!"

"Billy!"

"Mika!"

"Bil-" A familiar noise of a blade slashing freezes me in place. I recoil and the hand tugs me deeper into who knows where. I persist to fight them off scrambling for ideas to get us out of here. I fought and fought until I met the tip of Tracy's foot. To my dismay, I caught a glimpse of her sluggish body right as the officer flashed his flashlight over her. The blade cut cleanly.

I was too late.

"Gotcha you little runt!" The officer thunders, victoriously. "They're over here! At least two others!"

Following his voice, flashes of light dance across the leaves, disengaging my vision. The hand desperately reaches my waist and drags me into the void. I let out a scream and thrashed like a fish out of water. In doing so, a burning sensation grew within me.

"Stop struggling!" The voice commands. Their grip tightens and I let the electricity flow. It courses at my fingertips and exits out of the surface of my dermis, raising all the hairs on my body. "You're going to get yourself killed!"

Like a punching bag, the soldier's body swings away from me, hitting the tree trunk with high impact. He drops forward and collapses on his face beneath my boots. Luckily, I learned to wear them at all times, as I knew better than to let my guard down. They gave me the weight I needed to apply pressure on his back to hold him down.

Now, any senseless person would've run away into the dreary forest while their attacker was weak. Not me. I want to skin them alive and feed them to the wolves in the woods.

I wanted them to suffer.

It's not fair.

They took everything from me.

They killed Tracy. Who knows if they already killed Billy or-

I didn't allow myself to finish that thought.

"E-L-L" He mumbles in heavy breaths.

I pulled my pocketknife from the pocket of my boots. I could've picked any other weapon. A gun. A long string of rope. A pair of rusty scissors. A bomb.

But no.

They would've killed him too quickly. I wasn't so merciful, especially not since Max's passing.

Mika knew it.

Billy knew it.

Tracy knew it.

I knew it.

We've run this tendency of mine countless times. If it wasn't for the circumstances we were in, they probably would've considered me to be a serial killer. I sometimes see fear in the twin's eyes, especially Billy.

There was one occasion where I felt my anger surpass my empathy. Billy and I were searching for berries to pick, and we encountered an officer. I killed her without hesitation and stabbed her body thirty-seven times. Billy had stopped me at thirty-eight. "They're already dead." He comments, holding my wrist mid-air. We returned to camp together and didn't talk about it at all since then.

I effortlessly flick the pocket knife's blade open and bend down. He kept his face planted, taking a few more shaky breaths and mumbling the first letters of my name.

"E-L-E-" He gasps.

"Pathetic." I snicker a chuckle, running the tip close to his cheek reopening a familiar scar. Any idiot could've recognized him by that simple mark, but me, no. I was far too gone into my insanity to recall anything. I only permitted myself to the simplest of thoughts. Bloodshed. Survival. Mika.

"Maybe I should carve out your face." I threaten. "That will teach you a lesson or two."

A shadow towers next to me, urging me to hurry. Judging by the specks of lights trickling through the bushes, the officers would find us soon. I guess I can't take my time to torture him.

What a pity.

"Elen-n-n"

I move the blade further down his face and onto the tip of his chin. "Let me guess, cat caught your toun-"

The fading lights flicker directly on his face. A recognizable face. My eyes widen in horror causing me to take a step back from him. I don't say his name. Instead, a gasp escapes my lips.

Charles.

I retract my knife and allow him to lift himself up. With a shaky hand, he hooks his firm grip on my wrist and pulls me away from the oncoming officers emerging through the trees and bushes.

"Wait. I need to find someone." I spin my heels as we deviate from the river waters.

"They already got them." He replies swiftly, reeling me in his direction.

"W-w-what do you mean they got them?" I pull my wrist from him.

He snaps his head back at me and rubs his temple. "You'll understand soon."

"No!"

"El-"

"I said no! I am tired of being led around without being told anything. For all I know, you are leading me right into the hands of the G.C.P.O.A. That is unless you already are one of them."

"We do not have time for this!" he exclaims in a low voice.

"Then make time." I challenge.

He hauls a small object from his back pocket and tosses it blatantly at my feet. It bounces once and rolls over to a nest. A Nelly sat there staring at the object, prodding it slightly. I like to imagine she was testing the object for reassurance. I kneel and pick the object from the floor recognizing it immediately.

"Is that enough of an explanation?"

"She's alive?" I ask, careful to not let my static prints ruin the ridges of the ball. I wanted to hear it from him before I got my hopes up too high.

"They both are." He clarifies. "One of us found them picking at a berry bush during our night patrol. They were skeptical at first but the little one seemed to recognize me."

"So, when you said they already got them, you didn't mean the G.C.P.O.A, you meant,"

"The Homing Herd. Yes,"

The flickering lights intensified, scattering the branches and bushes like a couple of hound dogs. I was surprised they hadn't sent those to find us in the first place.

"And back there with my friend, Tracy? What about her?"

His expression darkened and so did mine. I didn't need a further explanation to know the rest. Rather than use my ability, I let the bomb do what I initially wanted it to do. I instructed Charles to step away, and when I felt them close enough, I held the button and set the bomb free. It soared past us and directly to the lights. Charles and I ducked to the ground and at my command, the bomb exploded. It took all that was left of my hearing out of my left ear. Though, I didn't mind. I didn't need to hear them to know how many I had killed. It was more than enough for me to see the world go dark.

Tracy was right, my vengeance wasn't as sweet as I'd like it to be. It didn't bring Maxine back, and it definitely wasn't going to do the same for her either. But it did one thing. It sent a message.

We are not kids meant to be trifled with.

34

As we made way to our destination, I thought about Tracy and how I had failed her. She had said my name, and I had fated her to walk with the Grim Reaper. If she had decided to haunt me alongside the others I have killed, I wouldn't complain. I cursed myself for her death, but then the smell of ash in the air reminded me of who the real killer was.

"We have to move quickly. More of them will be coming our way. The bomb can hold them off for so long." Charles mutters under his breath. I found it odd how he could talk to me so loosely. I thought my actions would drive him away or perhaps change his mind. Instead, he continued to regard me with sincerity and somewhat parental authority. He'd tell me to tie my boots whenever the laces became undone and casually checked if I was still there.

I nod and together we pick up our pace. The clock to our lifeline was ticking. Vainly, the sun made that evident. It snuck right behind us, past the horizon, and scattered its shadows among our footprints. You would think the light would bring anyone comfort, but instead, it did the opposite. I hated the sun. It took us away from the beautiful constellations that once kept us company.

Soon enough, as our toes burned, we eventually met up with one of Charles's comrades. She stood there waiting for us underneath a large tree, positioning her weapon at her side. She smiles with relief and tilts her head when she spots me.

"Are they?"

"Yes, they're both in the tunnels. They'll be there in no time," she replies. "And who are you, young miss?" She addresses me immediately.

"El." I coldly chided. She noticed my eyes locked on the gun she held at her hip and put it aside. Her finger curled pretentiously over the trigger.

"Well, El, you'll be safe soon. Both of your friends are waiting for you, but um, Charles, can I have a word?" She shifts her gaze over to him. Unlike when Charles was with Esmeralda, there was a stern level of professionalism between him and his comrade. It was clear they had been undercover for a while and were slowly losing hope.

"Anything you say to him, you can say to me," I grumble, frustrated with all the secrets and the constant unknowingness of my fate. My lack of sleep definitely influenced my state of irritability.

"El, I don't-"

"I've watched thousands of my friends die and blew up soldiers not long ago. Whatever you say to him, I can handle it. I'm not a child anymore."

"Yes. You are. We are the adults and-"

"And most of you have doomed us." I snap without a stutter. "I have kept my friends and I alive for the past few weeks with little to no optimism. If you're trying to save my hopes, forget it."

She keeps her gaze on Charles, having a silent exchange with him. They go back and forth, making slight gestures until they reach an agreement. "Very well." She sighs. "They're on our tail. If we don't go now, we'll lose our cover. As for the girl, why is there only one?"

"We lost the other one."

"Charles, what do you mean by lost? I promised the other two that their friends would be fine. I only see one." She asserts.

Charles rubs the back of his neck. This small subtle gesture was enough of a response. Her eyebrows furrowed with disappointment, as though she had heard this story far too many times. "I see." Her voice deepens.

She then turns to me with a mouthful of pity words waiting on her lips. I didn't want to hear it. Instead, I took over the narrative.

"My friend Tracy had her throat slit open. She won't be coming. How far do I need to go?"

"Not much. Continue straight until-"

"I'll take her there. You go back and cover for me."

"They're going to get suspicious."

"They already are Miranda." He utters. "I'll meet you back there once I drop her off."

Her eyes juggled between Charles and I, contemplating whether it was a good idea or not. "Fine. But you have exactly ten minutes. That's all I could give you."

"That's all I need," He attests, moving away from her. I follow behind him, running as best as I can to keep up with him. He doesn't waste another second of our delicate schedule. During our run, I found myself struggling to keep up. He was fast as lightning. Ironic, I know. It was almost laughable but not as laughable when we approached what seemed to be a flat area of the forest.

Charles started to do this weird thing where he would pat the bottom of his boot and be disappointed when the leaves made a crunch. It made me chuckle a few times despite the severity of our situation. To be fair, I was entirely sleep-deprived, hungry, delirious, and—oh what's the word I'm looking for? Right! Unhinged.

The fatigue still got to me as much as the thundering headaches. As for my body, the burns on my arms itched like crazy. I wanted to throw myself into the river to get rid of my growing pains. There was no doubt they wouldn't contribute to the rest of the other scars. They painted the surface of my dermis like a canvas. Each scar marked a terrible memory I've encountered.

Another thing to note about this part of the forest was the god-awful stench filling the air. I gagged a few times until I learned to tolerate it. It was an absolute shi-

Clunk!

Charles's face beams with excitement as he waves to me to get closer to him. I've never seen him have this much emotion on his face before. With great, and I mean great hesitation, I reluctantly stepped close to him, overwhelmed by the most awful thing to pierce my nostrils. "What the hell is that smell?" I say disdainfully, pinching my nose with my fingers.

"Sweet freedom."

I didn't know it would smell so awful. I always presumed freedom smelt like a fresh ocean breeze.

Getting on his knees, he rubs off a pile of dirt and leaves, revealing a large metal plate on the ground. He lifts the heavy plate and exposes me to an intensive version of the smell. Another gag rose in my throat.

"Go inside."

"You can't be serious." I gape, dumbfounded.

"Go. Inside." He commands.

At the edge of the dark sewage pipe is a ladder for me to climb down. "Once you get to the bottom, I want you to follow the walls."

"I beg your pardon?"

"Follow the walls with your hands to lead you to where you're supposed to be."

"And what about my friends?"

"You'll find them."

"How-" A static noise filled with a banshee's shriek pours out of the communication device Charles had at his belt. It sounded like Miranda. The whites of his eyes double in size as he hurries me inside.

"What's happening? Is Miranda okay?"

"We've run out of time. Hurry."

"Why don't you come with us?"

"Because someone has to cover the entrance. GO!" He roars, placing the metal plate over my head. The light was gone, and my grip tightened over the ladder. I wish I had checked how far down it went. I've lost count of each step.

Right foot. Left foot. Right foot. Left foot. Over and over making sure I wouldn't plummet to the bottom. When I felt bold, I extended my foot further to make faster progress and allowed myself to slide down.

BAM!

BOOM!

BAM!

BANG!

Something or *someone* drops on top of the metal plate causing a loud echo to flow inside the sewage tunnel. I quicken my pace and meet the bottom of the ladder. The noise persisted with a few more destructive rhythms. I did my best to ignore them and focused on getting the stench out of my nose. That is if it ever will. This place is disgusting. Drips of sewage hit my dermis with little to no warning. Some drops were less solid than others. I fought the urge to wipe it off as I knew that might cause risk for it to go on my hands.

Releasing the edge of the ladder, I place my right hand against the wall and start walking to what I think is straight. I took a wrong step and squished the tail of a rat. It howled with the echoes of the violence and fled away from me once I lifted my foot. Their scattering footsteps were barely audible, but I knew the creature was long gone. I bet it hated being down here as much as I do.

At least it was free. I thought to myself.

I found a speck of relief when I felt no debris hitting the nape of my neck. That must mean they have moved away from the tunnel. Charles's efforts were not lost after all. If he had been right, that must have meant Billy and Mika were down here somewhere. Out of precaution, I waited in silence for a few minutes before attempting to call them.

"Mika!"

No response.

"Mika it's me!"

Nothing.

"Billy? Billy, are you there?"

Sounds of footsteps linger near me. They weren't small enough to be Mika.

"Billy!" My voice rose to a clamor. Their footsteps trickle behind mine, only faster. It wasn't Billy. It couldn't be. He would've answered by now.

I shut my lips together doing the one thing I am good at, I run.

Shoot.

Shoot.

Shoot.

If Charles was genuine, he wouldn't lead me to a trap. Miranda said they were safe. I had to believe them. I *wanted* to believe them.

I kept my pace and thought about my next moves. If worst comes to worst, I'll use my ability. The downfall is like a star, when I explode, I burn and fall just as fast. One more try could knock me out. I had very few weapons to work with as my bag was still at our camp. Sure, there was the knife inside my boot, but I needed something more *accessible.* I didn't want to swing it in the dark and cut myself or let it be used against me.

Huff.

Their breath was over my shoulder. My fingertips buzzed with electricity as I braced myself for my attack. Like I expected they made their first move. They swung at me with an object in their hands, hitting my shoulder blade. Spinning towards them, I spout the beams out of my fingertips and burst a wave of electricity. They fall flat on their back and wince in pain. On the opposite side of the tunnel are several individuals racing directly at us.

"Stop!" yelps the voice.

Taken by surprise a sharp object strikes my side, matching the one on my shoulder. Another one follows hitting my arm. They weren't bullets. That I know. It replicated the pinch of a needle. I assume it had some kind of sedative as the tingling at my fingertips was fighting my command. A slight static formed, giving me little to nothing to work with.

"Come on!" I curse, letting what was left of my ability buzz inside of me.

"She's going to do it again!" shouts another voice at the opposite end.

"Hurry, re-load another!"

"I'm trying!"

"How is she doing that?"

"Don't shoot her!"

"She's going to electrocute us if we don't." replied what I think is a fourth person. They were barely audible compared to the others. It was far too disorientating, as my sight was as useless as my hearing.

I was very afraid. Scared out of my mind. A numbness sank in my knees, causing me to lose balance. Like a veil, a figure passes over my body. I didn't want to give them the chance. This time I didn't control it. If I was going to burn, I best be as bright as possible.

"AUGH!" I bellow. The voltage spewed inside my veins, extending into hissing flashes of Medusa's snakes, striking at whoever approached me.

35

It was quick. I was back in my backyard underneath the large fig tree, lying upside down on one of the branches I carved my initials on.

I **wasn't dead**. I could feel it. There was still a string of life connecting me to the other side.

On the tree, thousands of plump figs flourished on its branches, fruitful and unbothered by the gentle breeze. Standing on the opposite side was the one person who had been waiting for me. He remained smiling with his cat-green eyes. They glowed with such pensiveness and pain. It's not that he was *in* pain. It was that it pained him to see *me* disheveled like this.

The best way to describe myself is being as composed as a shipwreck. A few pieces of my metal exterior held me together despite the open seams inside of me. Maxine was the sea I had sunken into.

"Maxine," I gasp tearfully. Snot trailed at the tip of my lip, and my eyes puffed like clouds, but I didn't care. Here he was standing in front of me without bullets in his body. Nothing could've prepared me for this reunion. I thought if I had stayed awake all those nights, I would have been able to avoid this encounter. I didn't want it to be so soon despite missing him dearly. I was afraid he'd detest me for all that I have done and the people I have killed under his name. I failed him. Tracy. Everyone.

His frown deepened as though he was reading my mind. He jumps on his toes and picks a small fig. He hands the purple fruit over to me with nothing but reassurance. Seeing him now, I realized it wasn't his character to act in the way I presumed. My initial fear and anger had been a projection of myself.

"I-I-I'm so sorry Maxine." I hiccup, staring at the fig at his fingertips. I couldn't tell you a time when we didn't eat them together. They were going to be in season the day they took us.

"I'm sorry I couldn't protect you. I broke our promise and I-"

Swish.

The walls of my ship crumbled as another wave charged at me. "It should've been me! I should've died in the waterfall! Not you! Dios!"

I drop to my feet, digging the tips of my nails around my neck. The lump stopping my voice wouldn't go away.

He protectively inches closer to me, kneeling. I allow him to wrap his delicate arms around my head and pry my talons away from my collarbone. I wept alongside him; afraid he'd disappear the same way Xander did. I knew I had to come to my senses soon. After all, I had to set an example. Regardless of whether this was or wasn't my imagination.

Taking a few unsteady breaths, I straighten my spine and wipe my eyes to anchor myself at the bottom of the sea floor. The tides were shifting, and I didn't want to waste any more of it with my grief. I took the fig he had offered and told him to get one too. We clink them together like teacups and take a bite. I relished the sweet flavors and texture of the seeds.

Plop.

The ball slips out of my pocket and rolls at his feet. He doesn't pick it up. Rather, he steps aside and permits a small creature to peck at the ball's signature.

"Nelly!" I gasped. "You followed her!"

Seeing her brought me a speck of relief, knowing he wasn't alone. I lightly stroke her fur and let her play with Maxine's baseball. She chirped with glee and carried on.

"Max,"

He takes another bite from his fig.

"I never said this enough, but I love you so much. You are the best brother I could have, and I hope that someday, or somewhere, I'll be able to keep you safe. It looks like Nelly will have to do that in the meantime okay?"

He steadily moves his head, understanding what I am saying. As though he feels it too, a small tug reaches my wrist.

"I think I have to go now…" I hiccup, wiping some of the snot with my thumb. *"They need me."*

Maxine peacefully lowers his gaze and smiles in approval. He picks the ball up from Nelly and gently passes it to my freed hand. "Until next time," I say tucking the ball into its place.

"Promise?" He murmurs, lifting his finger.

I crouch to his level and link our pinkies. "I promise."

In unison, we snapped our fingers, and that was the end of him. The tugging persisted and I was back in my body. I recognized her blond pigtails as she hovered over my nose, underneath a bright light. A dark shadow towers over her and widens its mouth.

"El, where's Tracy?"

www.ingramcontent.com/pod-product-compliance
Lightning Source LLC
Chambersburg PA
CBHW070607300726
48975CB00006B/1736